Tilt

Tilt
Alan Cumyn

GROUNDWOOD BOOKS
HOUSE OF ANANSI PRESS
TORONTO   BERKELEY

Groundwood Books / House of Anansi Press
110 Spadina Avenue, Suite 801, Toronto, Ontario M5V 2K4
or c/o Publishers Group West
1700 Fourth Street, Berkeley, CA 94710

We acknowledge for their financial support of our publishing program the Canada Council for the Arts, the Government of Canada through the Canada Book Fund (CBF) and the Ontario Arts Council.

Canada Council   Conseil des Arts
for the Arts   du Canada

ONTARIO ARTS COUNCIL
CONSEIL DES ARTS DE L'ONTARIO

Library and Archives Canada Cataloguing in Publication

Cumyn, Alan
Tilt / Alan Cumyn.

ISBN 978-1-55498-119-9 (bound).—ISBN 978-1-55498-110-6 (pbk.)

I. Title.

PS8555.U489T54 2011   jC813'.54   C2011-902085-8

Cover photograph: Media Bakery
Design by Michael Solomon

Groundwood Books is committed to protecting our natural environment. As part of our efforts, this book is printed on paper that contains 100% post-consumer recycled fibers, is acid-free and is processed chlorine-free.

Printed and bound in Canada

For Suzanne

1

THE NEW GIRL came upon him un-
expectedly. He was alone in the dark parking lot
behind the auto-glass shop where nobody went at
night except for him. It was hard to explain what he
was doing. He was developing a twisting kick that
involved heaving himself into the air with a broom
handle. The kick part was coming along, but the
landing needed work.

He was picking little asphalt bits out of his knee
when she happened by.

"Hey," she said, not the least bit startled. Perhaps
she hadn't seen the kick. Still, he was a male in a
shadowy back alley developing his own secret martial art, and many girls would have been frightened
out of their boots.

She wasn't wearing boots. She was wearing

flip-flops that went *thwack thwack* with every step, and a pair of ordinary jeans and a light windbreaker. She was taller than him and big-shouldered. Her hair stood up at odd angles as if she hadn't slept in forty-eight hours and had then been electrocuted. It was red tonight, as far as he could see.

Janine. Janine Igwash.

Janine Igwash walked straight past him, then climbed the fence, which was eight feet high and topped with rusted barbed wire. No hesitation, gone so fast he wondered if he hadn't simply imagined her. Yet another absurdity of being sixteen. New girls bigger than him with weird hair appeared in the darkness and slithered up fences like feral ghosts.

He liked the sound of that: *feral ghosts*. What did it mean? He took out his notebook and wrote in the darkness, *she grazed my spine like a feral ghost*.

Maybe the beginning of a poem? He flipped back a page to *the perfect jump shot begins in the soul/ sole*. He could just read it by the dull light from the back wall of the auto-glass.

He imagined Janine Igwash walking past him again, only this time he was reading from his notebook. And instead of saying, "Hey," she said, "What's that?" Then he looked up at her coolly and said, "I keep track of my thoughts from time to time." Then she sat cross-legged beside him and he read to her snippets of his thoughts such as the one about the jump shot. And she said, "Really?" As if she'd never thought of it that way. And why would she have?

"My name is Stan," he said to her in this revised version happening in his head. "Most of the kids in school, they call me Stanley, but really it's Stan. I was the final man cut from the JV squad last year but this year I'm going to be a starter."

He got up then, picked up the basketball he had left in the shadows, bounced it twice then launched a beautiful arcing shot at the hoop he'd personally nailed, with backboard, to the old pine tree leaning up against the fence. *Swish*.

Out loud, to no one, to the feral ghost of Janine Igwash, he said, "With shots like that, I am going to be a starter."

Then he limped over to the spot on the fence where the girl had disappeared just minutes before. He pulled himself up the chain link. There was even a space in the rusty barbed wire that he could see would be almost easy to slither through. He peered into the darkness through the leaves.

She had just arrived late last year. It must have been hard for her coming into the school knowing nobody. Especially with a name like Igwash.

He was gazing across a backyard. Janine's? A light snapped on in an upstairs bedroom. Someone's shadow against the curtains. Spiky hair. Maybe she was about to undress, her silhouette black against the white screen. It was hard to see through the leaves, but it sure looked like she was tugging at her shirt.

He climbed down. His knee felt better. He snapped a few high kicks without the broom handle, then punched the air six times rapid-fire, a quick exhalation with each strike. Then he retrieved the basketball again and let loose a turnaround jumper without looking, entirely by feel. The ball hit the back of the rim, then the front, then the back, then spun out and bounced, the sound echoing down the dark alley.

The perfect jump shot begins in the soles of the feet. It moves like a wave through the calves and the thighs up to the hips and along the spine to the shoulder, elbow, wrist, hand and out the fingertips, a natural stroke as at ease in the universe as an ocean wave that curls and falls. Easier than breathing. Truer than thought.

Stan liked that. *Truer than thought.* He bounced the ball seven more times, pounding a single word into his brain—*starter, starter, starter*—then glanced again through the darkness at what he thought might be Janine Igwash's bedroom window.

———

HOME IN DARKNESS. Stan turned on the porch light as he slid past the squeaky screen door.

"Mom?" He kicked off his sneakers, left them with his basketball and broomstick in the hall closet. The kitchen was dark, too. "Mom?"

She was sitting in the den with three remotes on her lap and a glass of wine on the telephone table. The TV was dark. As soon as he entered, she thrust the remotes aside and picked up her wine glass. A binder lay open at her feet and the room smelled like work—like the worry of it.

She snapped it shut, as if she didn't want him to see something.

Budget Contingencies, the binder said.

"These two," Stan said, picking up the gray remote and the fat black one, "you never need to touch. Just leave them in the cabinet. Maybe I should label them?"

"How was your day, sweetie?" The red wine left a small line on top of her lipstick that he wished she would wipe off.

"The only one you need to use is this one." He held the skinny gray remote in front of her eyes at a reasonable focal distance. "And the only button you need to press is this one." He showed her the AUX button. Then he pressed it. Nothing. "Unless somebody has been hitting buttons randomly. Then you have to press the Satellite button."

She pretended to be watching. "Did you get something to eat?"

"I had the chicken salad, and I fed Lily, too. This button here. It says 'satellite.' We only have to press that once in our lives, then never again. The remote remembers."

His mother picked up the binder and began to flip through densely printed pages.

"The remote remembers," he said again, in case it might make a difference. He pressed the Auxiliary button and the TV sprang to life. A couple danced frantically in feathered spandex.

"There's nothing on anyway," she said. "I was just waiting for Gary."

Gary, Gary, Gary. Stan turned off the dancers. He picked up the two extra remotes and put them in the back of the TV cabinet.

"Is he coming over or something?" It was hard to keep the curdle from his voice.

"He said he was going to call. I'm not going out. I have an eight o'clock tomorrow morning." Stan's mother finished her wine and sat in her very still way, as if inviting the mossy green of the sofa to slowly take her over. Her hand remained on the binder, but her eyes were glassy with fatigue.

Stan walked into the kitchen and performed his own meditation in front of the open fridge. The carton of organic grapefruit juice stared back. He pulled it out and looked for a date: *26 Sep*. No wonder it had tasted fuzzy that morning.

Water at the tap. Stan twisted to drink. When he straightened up, his mother's phone rang.

"Oh, it's you," Stan heard her say from the other room in that girly voice she only used when talking to Gary.

Up the stairs. Stan practiced walking with his weight channeled to the outside of each foot to transfer the force of every step smoothly, like a soundless wave. Step number five was impossibly squeaky. But if the footfall were in the exact resonance of the loose board . . .

"Well, you always have the same idea," his mother said downstairs.

Into Lily's room. The floor too had a resonance he tried to feel with his feet. Little girl sleeping, her wild hair everywhere on the pillow. She was clutching Mr. Strawberry by the neck and already clenching her jaw.

Stan turned out her light and she opened her eyes.

"Is Mommy going out?"

"No. Did you have a pee?"

"Did she tell you she wasn't going out?"

"I want you to have a pee."

"I don't need to."

"Yes, you do. Get up." Stan pulled at her wrist. She hit him feebly on the arm with Mr. Strawberry.

He marched her into their mother's bathroom. It still reeked of Chanel from some days before when Lily had run amok. A gift from Gary.

"I hate going in here," she said.

"Just plug your nose and go." Stan waited outside the door and tried not to look at the unmade bed, the scattered clothes. Gary's toothbrush for some reason lay on the bedside table.

"Nothing is coming!" Lily announced.

"Concentrate!"

The thin layer of dust on the dresser, on the closet mirror, on the abstract male nude hanging tilted over the bed.

"It's not coming!"

His mother's footfalls shuddered the stairs. How

could such a skinny woman make so much noise? When she thudded into the bedroom, her blouse was already half off.

"Oh, you're here," she said. But the blouse came all the way off anyway. Black lace bra.

Stan studied his toes. She slid open the closet door and flipped through her dresses as if they were files in a cabinet.

"Lily is peeing," he said.

"It's not coming!"

Stan's mother stepped out of her slacks, which stayed squatted on the floor in front of the closet.

Stan escaped to his bedroom. Even with the door closed and the pillow over his head he still heard Lily say, "But you said you weren't going out!" He plugged in his music. Gain/Loss sang, *Whatcha gonna do? Whatcha gonna do? Whatcha gonna gonna gonna gonna gonna do?* straight into his ears in the darkness over and over until the house was still.

Music off. Lily made little unasleep huffing-chuffing breathing noises in the next bedroom. He hadn't heard the door close, but his mother was gone. All still and dark.

With his eyes shut he imagined himself on the tryout court, all last year's returning JV stars there,

Coach Lapman watching, everyone watching. He caught the ball and leaned left, went right then *bing!* On the spot, straight up like a human spring . . . the wave moving through him, the spin of the ball, the arc in the air. *Swish*. Nothing but net. Nothing but window. Silhouette. Dark against light. The twisting shot . . . and the twist of Janine's arms as she tugged up the T-shirt . . . he hadn't looked and yet the black and white danced in his mind . . . her dark bra, the points of her hair, the fall of her breasts . . . despite it all the show went on as soon as he closed his eyes.

On and on it went.

2

THE ALARM. Seven a.m. Stan was somewhere in the mountains fighting off a band of terrorists intent on stealing all the mountain goats. They were falling to his broom handle, to his furious feet.

Then he was awake and stiff. Stiff as a guy wire.

It made no sense at all. He stared up at the gloomy ceiling waiting to unstiffen.

He lifted his knees so that the sheets would touch nothing. Emptied his mind. Filled it with dishes. Dust mops. Digging in the garden. Foot on shovel. Shovel in dirt. Worms wriggling in black earth. Limp, cold, squishy earthworms.

Ridgepole.

Stan got up. Ridgepole in his pajamas. Why?

He pulled on a sweatshirt, snuck to the door and glanced out. Silence, all clear. He eased down the stairs, keeping his weight on the outside of each foot.

"Stanley?" His mother was at the front door. Just coming in.

Stan sat on the stairs, pulled his legs together and the sweatshirt down.

"How's Gary?" he asked.

His mother fiddled with her shoes in the front hall. She never wore heels except when she saw Gary. And her dress barely made it halfway down her thighs.

"I thought you have an eight o'clock?" Stan said.

"I do. I do!" Now she wanted to get by him on the stairs. "Are you all right, honey?"

Stiff as a poker. Erect as the Washington Monument.

"I just have a little stitch in my side," he said.

"Oh, honey."

"I'm going to sit here like this until it goes away."

"Maybe you should walk around a bit."

"I'm just going to stay exactly like this." Stan squished over to the side of the step so that his mother could get by.

"Do you want some orange juice?"

"No."

"Sometimes drinking something—"

"I'll be fine. You need to get going."

She squeezed past finally. Stan went into the bathroom and stood over the toilet. From the upstairs he heard his mother say, "Oh, Lily!" again and again. He heard sheets being pulled off the bed, his mother's heavy footfalls, Lily's crying. His mother's voice became operatic. "I just don't understand. If you need to get up in the night, get up! I know you peed before—"

"I just didn't feel it! I just didn't . . ."

Now his mother was calling down the stairs.

"Stanley, could you please handle your sister's sheets? I have an eight o'clock!"

Life was better down in the basement. It was dark and cool and the ceiling was low enough that Stan could almost bump his head. Maybe by Christmas he would bump his head. And quiet. No amount of opera from upstairs could leak all the way down into the basement, especially when the washing machine was running.

It only took a minute to dump in the sheets and soap and set everything going, but Stan stayed for the pure peace of it. He liked the smell of the detergent. House in order. He leaned against the machine.

Janine Igwash walked out of the darkness again right past him. She lingered near him in silence by the laundry table where the old spent sheets of fabric softener congregated along with little bits of tissue left in pockets from laundries past.

The temperature went up inexplicably. It was a cold-water wash but the heat was on. She was just by the laundry table, breathing. He leaned a little harder against the washing machine. She was bigger than him but not by much. She started to tug at her T-shirt. Arms crossed at the bottom the way women do. Breathing and . . .

Stan stepped back. Leaning up against the washing machine! He opened the lid and watched the cold soapy gray water churn, churn, churn until it was safe to head upstairs again.

———

JANINE IGWASH SAT four rows away from him in biology. She was wearing a red shirt that his eyes had trouble keeping buttoned, especially once he noticed a small tattoo at the base of her neck near her shoulder. He wasn't close enough to see what it was. She didn't look at him at all.

They were dissecting cows' eyes but there weren't enough eyes to go around, thank God, so they were in groups of four. Jason Biggs was handling the scalpel. Taking notes were the identical sisters Melinda and Isabelle Lafontaine who were each wearing jeans and pearls and running shoes. One of them was pierced in the left eyebrow, the other in the right. Stan could never keep them straight. They both had big watery eyes like this sorry specimen Jason Biggs was slicing apart.

"Stop now, Jason!" Left Eyebrow said. "I think we're supposed to sketch that."

Janine Igwash turned and pulled her red shirt off her shoulder. Stan's mind could make her do that. But he still couldn't quite see the tattoo.

"Lapman canceled junior varsity for this year," Jason Biggs said then.

Janine unbuttoned a bit more and pulled her shirt farther off her milky white shoulder and stepped toward him, parting the desks . . .

"What?"

Her tattoo was something sinewy, coiled but not a snake, prettier and . . .

Biggs snapped his fingers. "Canceled!"

Gray desiccated flesh hung off the pitiful eyeball.

"How can he do that?"

"He just did. They couldn't find another coach. Lapman is doing girls' JV this year. You'll have to try out for Burgess."

Burgess, the varsity coach, ate juniors for breakfast.

"You can keep going, Jason," Right Eyebrow said. "Let's get the cross-section."

"*Lapman's coaching girls' JV?*" Stan said. He felt his gut contract into a hard rubber ball. *No JV?* After he had trained on his own, night after night, month after month . . .

"Weren't you the final guy cut last year?" Biggs said. "You should have made it, man."

This felt like one of those bits of news that was going to take a long time to comprehend. Like when his father left five years ago to live with the twenty-three-year-old he had impregnated. That could not be understood all at once. Stan didn't feel like he understood most of it even now. It took time to soak down through the layers, like water working its way through clay.

He hadn't seen his father since.

"No way you should have been cut. Towers is a pretty good guard but he can't shoot. I've seen you shoot, man." Biggs looked up like a doctor in the middle of some surgery and said to the twins, "This guy never misses. I've never seen him miss."

"It's about time we had a junior varsity for the girls," Left Eyebrow said.

Stan's hands flexed as if holding the pebbled

grain of an imaginary basketball. Now what was he supposed to do? Varsity only had two spots open. Everyone else was coming back. Now there would be twelve from last year's JV competing for those two spots—all right, eleven. Collins broke his leg skateboarding. But what about all the seniors who didn't make varsity last year?

Suddenly Janine Igwash loomed above him. Completely clothed. Her tattoo was just a little red and black blob near the creamy white corner of her collar.

"What are you doing about the retina?" she asked him. Even though Jason Biggs was the one with the scalpel in his hand mucking about with the retina and who knew what else.

"We sketched it before we sliced it," Right Eyebrow said.

"I didn't think we were supposed to slice it," Janine Igwash said to him directly again. Her eyes were dark green with little brown blobs that flashed with light.

She looked down at the hatchet job Jason Biggs was doing, and back to Stan, and down and back again.

"There's this dance that my parents' youth group has forced me to help organize," she said to Stan. "And I'm supposed to go and it's like there's no possible way out of it in any way and, there's this stipulation." She shoved her hands in her pockets.

Was she really saying this? Stan went through a mental checklist. Everyone else was listening; she was wearing all her clothes. Probably it was real.

"Stipulation?" he said.

"I need to bring, like, a guy." She stood very still and looked at him, her green and browns scanning his face. Jason Biggs was most of the way through the eye now.

Someone kicked Stan's ankle. It was Left Eyebrow.

"A guy?" Stan said.

Janine Igwash couldn't seem to say anything more. Left Eyebrow kicked him again.

"Ten minutes, people, before you need to clean up," Mr. Stillwater announced. He was sitting at the front in the same blue shirt he wore every day, or maybe he had a whole closet full of blue shirts.

When Stan glanced at Janine Igwash again she was back at her station cleaning up. Her face was redder than her hair.

"You sure blew that one," the twins said together.

THE REST OF THE DAY slid by in jagged fragments, during which Stan heard again and again the unbelievable news about JV. Everyone seemed to know, maybe through Biggs, what the disaster meant to Stan personally. He thought he'd been secret about his obsessive practice.

But this was a complete crash and burn.

Once he caught sight of Janine Igwash at her locker on the second floor reaching for something on the top shelf amidst a bird's nest of squashed papers and other items. She certainly didn't need his help reaching the top shelf. But if she turned in the next second and a half he was sure he would stop and accept her invitation to the dance, if in fact it had been an invitation. When she did turn he was already almost past her.

Then later at lunchtime in the cafeteria lineup he pretended to be extremely interested in the new student mural of various androgynous figures playing sports such as hockey, soccer, volleyball and even basketball, although the basketball player had one arm longer than the other and his or her elbow was definitely out of alignment given the shoulder angle of the jump shot if in fact it was a jump shot that the artist was trying to depict, and what did it matter anyway now that JV was canceled?

Then there she was again at the end of second period in the afternoon, tying her shoe right in front of him as he was trying to make it to English and nearly tripped over her but fortunately his reactions were swift and he managed to miss her completely although she did look up at the last moment to see who was bearing down on her with such speed.

"Hey," he said as he flashed by.

It occurred to him that if he stopped he might say even more than that, but what?

In the hallway Coach Lapman didn't meet Stan's eye, probably didn't even remember who he was.

At home after dinner he was reading the same assigned passage of *The Catcher in the Rye* over and over when his mother approached. She sat quite close to him on the sofa so that he had to pull out his earbuds and turn off his music.

"Aren't you training tonight?" she asked.

"They canceled JV basketball," he said. Under questioning he explained the hopelessness of the situation.

"Well, you could try out for the varsity team anyway, couldn't you?" she said.

Stan knew that if he just stayed quiet she would eventually drift away and he could get back to not reading his novel. Anyway, Gary would be calling soon.

She squeezed his knee in a motherly way.

"How are things on the other side?" she asked.

"What other side?"

"The social side of things. Any . . ." His mother hesitated so he knew she had probably been planning this segment of the conversation all along. ". . . cute girls, you know, you're interested in?"

"Cute girls?"

"You know what I'm saying, Stanley." She stretched flat her brow furrows with her fingertips.

"I guess," Stan said.

"What do you guess?"

She was almost finished her wine. Gary was going to call any minute. Or Lily was going to need help with her homework. If he could just stall a bit longer . . .

"We haven't had any good conversations about all this," his mother said. She waved her hand vaguely. "I'd like to think that you feel free enough to ask me anything. You're entering such a rich and . . . confusing time of life. And your father isn't here to help. It's just me. You know I grew up with sisters, so I really don't know the male perspective . . . I know men, of course . . . I know I'm terrible with them. I'm really not much of a role model for you. But if there is anything you want to talk about . . . you know, the mechanics of . . . how it all works." The words were sputtering now. Not even the wine was helping. "You do know the mechanics?"

He couldn't avoid the direct question.

"We had a . . . mechanics section as part of health," he said.

"But you haven't . . ." She squeezed his knee again. Her hair was falling all in front of her face.

Where was Gary when you needed the guy?

"Haven't what?" Stan said finally.

"You know . . . you haven't actually . . . I mean, you do go out at night sometimes. And I know I'm away more than I should be. I mean—"

She was asking if he'd—!

"*No!*" he blurted.

She looked startled. Surprised and relieved and perhaps disbelieving.

"It's all right if you do. I mean, eventually, when you love someone. I mean, not now, but in the next few years you're going to be entering an age when the feelings are overpowering and . . . there's the whole thing about the adolescent brain."

"*What?*"

"I was reading about this. The center for consequences is underdeveloped . . . I mean, in the adolescent brain . . ."

At last, the phone! Stan felt his shoulders ungrip.

But it wasn't his mother's phone, it was the home line.

Lily picked it up then screamed, "Stanley!"

Nobody ever called him.

"It's for you!"

It was Janine Igwash. Stan didn't recognize her voice at first and was convinced someone was calling from across the continent to try to sell him something—tickets to a dance. But she wasn't selling, she was asking.

"I know I sounded like a stammering clownface this morning in biology but what I was trying to get out was it's Saturday night. This Saturday. It starts at eight o'clock and I don't think I would stay past ten or so and we don't even have to dance if you don't want to. I mean, there will be music and such. But if you don't like to dance then we could just, I don't know, hang out." She paused. "Feel free to jump in and say something any time about now."

Stan considered his words. His mother poured herself another glass of wine not ten feet away and pretended she wasn't listening.

"We don't have to worry about transportation because my parents will be driving. I think maybe I mentioned this is their thing. Are you still there? You do talk, don't you?"

"Sure," Stan said.

"Well?"

"I just, uh, I'm not sure why you're asking *me*?"

Stan's mother chopped something hard on the counter so that he dropped the phone. When he picked it up he said, "Sorry about that," but it was into a dial tone.

3

AT 2:17 A.M., after precisely no sleep, Stan snuck downstairs, bypassed squeaky stair number five and, sitting in the den on the couch near the window by the light of the streetlamp outside, composed the following letter to Janine Igwash:

I know you think I'm an idiot. But I have never been asked out before by any girl so I guess it's not surprising I didn't know how to act. I've been training for something . . . different and now that's been canceled and sometimes it's hard to change gears.

Also, I'm not a usual sort of guy. I feel like I'm older than that in some ways. Maybe when I *am* older I'll go completely off the road and behave just like a teenager but right now I don't want any part of the stupidity that is happening.

Maybe it's a drag your parents make you help organize things like youth dances but at least that means they have their own lives together. My parents are a complete mess. My father specifically doesn't live here anymore.

So I guess what I'm saying is that I'm trying really hard not to be 16. Does that make any sense?

One thing maybe it would be stupid to tell you but here I am writing it anyway is that I do think of you from time to time, and not just because you tried to ask me out. I do think of you.

But I don't want to be physical until I know how to be. Sexual I mean. I'm sorry for saying it.

I know you just asked me to a dance and even then you said I didn't have to dance. So maybe instead we'd go for a walk and I would tell you a lot of things. Maybe you have things on your mind too. It doesn't mean at all we would end up being physical but the problem would be afterward and mostly in my head but also in my body which is doing weird things. I may look like something on the surface but underneath a lot of the time I'm just barely clinging.

So going to the dance with you would be a lot bigger event than maybe you're thinking about.

Now it's almost 4 o'clock in the morning and I'm going to be a zombie if I don't go to bed. I'm sorry for my handwriting. I'm sorry if I actually give you this letter. I'm having one of those moments when I seem to be standing outside looking at myself wondering what I'm going to do and not having the slightest idea.

Yours sincerely,
Stan (Stanley) Dart

Stan folded the letter—six sheets of his miserable handwriting—three times, shoved it in the kitchen garbage, got halfway up the stairs, then turned around and pulled the letter out of the garbage. He took it upstairs to his room and stuck it under some papers at the bottom of his own wastebasket which only got emptied once a month at most. Then he pulled himself between the sheets.

Janine Igwash was instantly in his head, standing quite close to him though turned slightly away, looking down. She had dropped a button and was just about to bend over to look for it. Her black silky shirt was almost falling open, and the little tattoo at the base of her neck nearly peeked at him.

She was in his head like she was living there. The black shirt falling so softly off her shoulders, undone. Shirt tails. Off the rails. Light blue underwear the color of the sky. His heart hammering and all he was doing was lying there, still as a board. Stiff as a post.

Holding up the sky.

4

STAN SPIED THE TINY notice on the bulletin board outside the gym. *Tryouts for the boys' varsity basketball team begin Monday at 6:30 a.m.*

How could information of such vital importance be so sparse in detail? Thin blue ink, easy to miss. Maybe Coach Burgess was hoping no one new would show up. He only had two spots to fill anyway.

Six-thirty in the morning!

But instead of driving people off, the awkward start time only seemed to pique more interest. Marty Wilkens, who could barely tie his own shoes, said he was going to come out. He'd grown six inches over the summer and so maybe he might be able to play basketball. Leonard Palin, a hockey player, announced he'd been working on a left-handed hook shot. "It's unstoppable," he said in the hallway outside geography.

But really that hallway was owned by the enormous Karl Brolin, six feet six, 220 pounds of senior orangutan who flicked illegal bounce passes to Ty Blake and Jamie Hartleman, the core of the varsity team. No teachers told them to take it outside. They ran, jumped, pivoted, ricocheted off the lockers while Stan and others let them pass.

That's the way it was with those guys. Once last year at lunchtime Stan tried to guard Karl Brolin when Brolin decided to play at the junior basket outside just because he could. Brolin got the ball and backed in—backed in with his big rump and his huge shoulders until he was underneath the basket. Then, as now, all Stan could do was give way.

Stan carried his Janine Igwash letter—he'd retrieved it from the wastebasket—in an outer pocket of his backpack where it was zipped and sealed secure. He didn't want her to see it and so he kept it with him at all times.

Janine walked past him talking with Katherine Loney. Janine was a head taller than Katherine, though she didn't slouch like some tall girls did. He held the fire door but Janine did not glance at him. She simply kept listening as Katherine said, " . . . pieces of it everywhere, even in her hair!" If Janine had glanced over, Stan was prepared to say, "I'm sorry, I dropped the phone." His jaw was relaxed, the words were lining up, then she was by. Coldly, Stan thought. Determined not to look. "But why in her hair?" Janine asked. Stan didn't hear the reply. He was headed in the other direction. Nearly running.

To hell with her.

In the break after first period he sat underneath the stairwell at the south end of the building and wrote in tiny script at the bottom of page six of his letter to Janine: *what we cannot know/in the chaos of control.* He looked at those two lines—minutes were draining away, he was going to have to head to biology soon—and finally he scratched out the lines and added, *Why is everything so difficult?*

He didn't have a good sense in his head of how he was ever going to make the varsity team. There were too many good players. The players were too big, too strong, too experienced. All year he'd been imagining making his shots against the JV guys. But most of them were not going to make the varsity team, either.

In biology Jason Biggs said, "Tryouts for varsity start Monday at 6:30 in the morning!" They were supposed to be finishing their diagrams of the components of the eye. Janine Igwash did not look around once in the first ten minutes of the class.

"Six-thirty in the morning!" Jason Biggs said.

She was working on her diagram. If Stan's letter wasn't safely back in his locker he would have just walked up to her and handed it over. Simple as that. He felt like a man of action.

"Monday morning!" Jason Biggs said. "You gotta go, man. I've seen your jump shot. You never miss."

Then he looked to where Stan was looking.

"Not Janine Igwash," he said.

"What?"

"Everyone knows she's tilted."

Mr. Stillwater stopped talking and looked directly at the two of them.

"What does everyone know, Stanley?" he said.

Stan's ears were burning. They always gave him away. Biggs looked innocent as grass.

"What does everyone know?" Mr. Stillwater repeated. All eyes were on Stan.

"Nothing," Stan muttered.

"Everyone knows nothing?" Mr. Stillwater said.

Stan stayed silent. He sneaked a glance at Janine Igwash. Her face was pale, pale white, but her neck was red. Her hair was so wild he wanted to get lost in it.

What did Biggs mean by tilted?

"Stand up." Mr. Stillwater's eyes never left Stan. Maybe this wasn't going to pass after all. Stan rose uneasily. "What does everyone know?" Stillwater pressed.

"That I'm an idiot," Stan said. Janine laughed. She was the only one.

"Are you?" A little less heft in Stillwater's voice. The moment seemed suddenly open to comic possibilities.

"I'm talking with my idiot friend when I should be listening," Stan said. Some giggles now. "That makes me an idiot, too. I'm sorry, Mr. Stillwater."

Stillwater nodded slightly, his eyes narrowed.

"And sometimes I drop the phone when someone wonderful is on the other end," Stan continued. He looked directly at Janine, whose eyes were dark now—how did that happen? Black jewels. "And I fail to apologize because of just how awkward everything is at this age." Gales of laughter. Jason Biggs' desk nearly tipped over, Stan was leaning so hard against it. But Janine kept looking.

"That's enough. Sit down, Stanley!"

Stan sat down. Janine kept looking. He would not look away first. His heart was hammering. He was breathing like he was carrying a load of bricks up a tree for some reason.

Just because it had to be done.

Trumpets were blowing in the back of his head. He wanted to be at the dance right now.

To hell with varsity.

But biology wasn't over. Stan was in his seat. Janine Igwash was still across the room.

He had to wait while Mr. Stillwater filled the board with the definitions of the ciliary muscle, the optic chiasm, the lens, the iris, the fiber radiations.

Stan poked Jason Biggs on the shoulder.

"What do you mean she's tilted?" he whispered.

Stan borrowed some colored pencils from the twins. Pink for muscle. Yellow for ligaments. Blue for the iris, gray for the lens.

"She's a gwog," Biggs whispered harshly. Stan wasn't sure he had heard properly.

"A what?"

Janine's neck was white now, her face red.

"Tilted," Jason Biggs said again. "She's a tilted gwog."

Mr. Stillwater stood beside both their desks, looking with too much interest at their diagrams.

"Mr. Dart," he muttered eventually. "Did you never learn to color inside the lines?"

———

"SO YOU'RE AN IDIOT?" she said an eternity later, when they were outside biology.

"Total."

She smiled. God. How had he ever stood up in class like that?

"The dance is at eight o'clock. My parents are driving. You're going to have to meet them. They're, like, organizing the whole thing. Unless you have your license?" Her voice held a hopeful note.

Stan had his learner's permit. That was all. Why didn't he have his license yet? He'd been sixteen for almost three months. Every couple of weeks his mother took him out in the back lot and ground her teeth while he wrestled with the gearshift. He had a lot of trouble balancing between the clutch and the gas. He'd be a snap with an automatic, but they didn't own an automatic. Why didn't they own an automatic? They owned a rusting old stick shift because they were poor, poor because of the divorce.

Because of the weirdness of his family he didn't have his license yet, and so he was embarrassed in front of Janine Igwash.

"I don't have mine, either," she said. "But we have to go early because of my parents. Why don't you come by at a quarter after seven?"

Stan nodded. Why couldn't he speak around her?

He tried to smile but it felt as if his face was cracking. He was holding his jaw in the wooden way of everyone in his family.

All the others were gone from biology now. Stan needed to go somewhere else, too. Where? He hadn't the slightest idea.

Why didn't he have his license?

"You know where my house is?" Janine Igwash said.

Stan nodded. Then she was gone and he was standing on his own with the whole world swirling around him. What day was it? Nothing was in his head, so he had to look it up. This was Day Five and he had just finished biology — he was doing the hell out of biology — and so the next period was . . .

A note fell out of his grasp.

Why was he grasping a note?

The ringers rang. The hallway was empty. He was alone with his empty head, reading a note that said in Jason Biggs' stupid handwriting: *tilted=GWOG=goes with other girls=Janine Igwash=everybody else knows, ok?*

5

TILTED. JANINE IGWASH liked girls. Nothing wrong with that. Stan liked girls, too. He liked Janine. Girls with soft secret flesh, half-hidden tattoos. Visions of them roaming around his head.

Tilted.

She wanted him to go to the dance with her. As a front. An untilted front for her parents. That's as much as he could make out.

Tilted tilted tilted. All the way home.

Where he met Gary lying in the dirt of the driveway scratching something on the underside of his silver Audi with his fingernail. His beige jacket had fallen open, as had his light blue shirt—it looked like Mr. Stillwater's shirt. Buttons were open where his pink belly peeked out like mushroom flesh starved for the sun. *Shroomis gigantis.*

In private his mother pressed herself against this man's skin.

Gary twisted on his back, rubbed his elbow into the dusty asphalt.

"Hey, Gary." Stan stepped around his mother's boyfriend.

"I caught something on that speed bump near the auto wash," Gary said.

The car was gleaming even more than usual. Another stick shift. Stan wouldn't be able to drive it very well, either.

"I think my strut got bent," Gary said.

"Tilted?" Stan kneeled down but he couldn't see anything.

"It might affect the alignment," Gary said. He brushed himself off and for a moment the two were uncomfortably close.

Did Stan's mother really like that aftershave?

"How's school going?" Gary asked.

"Just great," Stan said.

———

STAN WAS HELPING Lily with her homework before dinner. She was adding columns of numbers:

28
+17
3051

"I don't know how you're getting that," Stan said.

"I'm just following," Lily said.

"Following what?"

"Two plus one is three," Lily began. "Carry the zero—"

"Wait, wait, wait! First of all, you start on the right, not the left. Eight plus seven is what?"

"That's not what Ms. Hennigan said!"

"You probably weren't listening. The column on the right is the ones column."

"Eight plus seven isn't *ones* at all!" Lily said.

Gary and his mother were downstairs in the kitchen getting dinner together. Stan heard Gary say, "I've never seen anybody slice tomatoes that way." Stan's mother said, "What way?" and Gary said, "Like you'd rather be squashing grapes."

It was a Gary joke. Stan didn't hear his mother laughing.

"On the right is the ones column, and on the left is the tens column. What's eight plus seven?" Stan asked.

"Fifteen! But then you carry the one to the other

side of the five." She traced over the 51 she'd written on the page.

Stan took the pencil from her. "Don't make stuff up. You carry the one up to the tens column, up here." He made a mark by the two. He was trying to stay calm.

"Ms. Hennigan has a different way. Just leave me alone!" She grabbed back the pencil and started an elaborate doodle on the edge of her page.

"You're going to burn the garlic!" Gary said down in the kitchen.

"No, I'm not," Stan's mother snapped. Something smelled like it was burning.

"You are, you are!" A pan clanged and hissed.

"I wonder how old he is now?" Lily murmured, almost to herself.

"Who?"

"Feldon!"

Stan's palm hit the desk. Lily jumped in her seat. *"Don't* mention his name!"

"Feldon Feldon Feldon Feldon!" Lily said. "The *baby!*"

Quiet down below. Not even cupboards banging. Stan remembered when his mother and father fought. The silence was the worst. His father had a volcanic temper.

"Feldon is five years old by now," Stan said.

"He's not a baby. Don't even think about him, or Dad, or anybody. All right?" Stan took his sister's head in his hands and turned it back to the figures in the notebook. "You start on the right, carry the one up here to the tens column, add one plus two plus one. What's it come out to?"

As soon as he let her go, Lily's doodle turned into a swirly *F* on the side of her paper. Her elbow nudged the textbook and a folded letter stuck out.

"What's this?" Stan said. He grabbed the paper and held it high so Lily could not reach it.

Dear parents/guardian. It was from the school. *It has recently come to our attention that your son's/ daughter's academic standing has slipped below the acceptable school board standard . . .*

"What have you done now?" Stan asked.

"Nothing," Lily said.

Stan scanned the rest of the letter. The principal was asking for a meeting.

"Is this about marks or something else?"

Lily laid her face on the open book now, clasped her hands over her head as if expecting bombs.

Still not another sound from the kitchen. Stan got up and listened by the bedroom door.

Silence was the very worst. He remembered his father with his fists doubled . . .

"*Mmm*," his mother sighed.

Great. Stan clomped down the stairs with the letter in his hand.

The air was thick with the smell of something burnt. Garlic? A stove element glowed red with nothing on it. Smoke curled up from the blackened pan that was resting in the sink.

His mother and Gary stood guilty, clenched in the middle of the kitchen, his upper lip and part of his chin smudged with her lipstick.

"Did you see this?" Stan handed the letter to his mother, whose face blanched. From upstairs he could just hear a tiny muffled voice, Lily singing, "*And little baby Feldon was his name.*"

"Shit for crackers," his mother said.

———

AT DINNER STAN PUSHED creamy linguine, only some of the garlic blackened, around with his fork. Gary wiped his plate with the white Italian bread Stan's mother never bought unless Gary was coming. Lily slurped the noodles until creamy sauce caked the wispy edges of her dangling hair.

"Well, it's not the end of the world," Stan's mother said. "We've met with the principal before."

"It's a different one," Lily said. "It's a *she*."

"Stanley will come with me," his mother said. She didn't have to say, *Stanley keeps me from weeping on principals' desks*. She didn't have to say, *Stanley makes the family appear reasonable*.

Stan's mother lunged across the table and wiped Lily with her napkin. Lily squirmed—Stan knew she would—and got even more of her hair in the sauce. Water splashed from two or three glasses but Gary managed to catch the wine bottle before it tipped.

"I just want to keep your hair out of dinner," Stan's mother said. She smiled at Gary—a frantic sort of near-mad gesture—and Gary reached across and touched her hand. That was all. Somehow because Gary touched Stan's mother's hand, Lily stayed still long enough to be wiped.

"You should wear your barrettes," Stan's mother said to Lily.

"Rachel Edmundson has them," Lily said.

Stan's mother didn't take the bait.

"Then just tie your hair back." She slid her glass over a few inches and Gary topped it up.

Stan had a memory of his father pouring wine, and then he and Stan's mother got up and danced slowly in the middle of the living room still holding their long-stemmed glasses. His mother's face fit perfectly into his father's shoulder.

They were happy sometimes. It wasn't all scream and sulk.

"She's a girl principal," Lily said.

"That doesn't mean you can just go along making up answers to all your assignment questions," Stan said, unable to hold himself back. "At some point you have to deal with reality." Stan looked to his mother for support, but she seemed to be at the end of her energy for coping with Lily.

"Sometimes reality is overestimated," she sighed. She could go that way, become limp and unparental in the flick of a moment.

Stan studied his plate and decided to stay quiet. They ate in unbearable silence until finally Gary made a point of asking Stan what was happening at school. So Stan told him, in as few words as possible, about the cancellation of JV.

"So you're a basketball player," Gary said.

Stan's mother chimed in. "Stanley used to play hockey but then suddenly that was all over. Now it's basketball."

She said it as if she'd really forgotten why he gave up hockey.

"I used to play basketball," Gary said improbably.

"I did, I did! We should play horse sometime. I've got a wicked jump shot." Gary stroked the air with his meaty hand. His belly rubbed against the table, and Stan grabbed two of the water glasses before they could spill again.

"You two should play!" Stan's mother said. She pressed Stan with her eyes, the way that she did now a hundred times a day over everything from wiping up the kitchen to taking out the garbage to helping Lily wrestle with the world.

Stan and his father used to play hockey. After school in the winters, out on the frozen rink in the park in the next neighborhood over.

Stan had not played hockey, had not skated, in five years.

But now Stan allowed that he would play Gary at horse any time. Gary said that he would like that, and Stan's mother's eyes said that she would like that, too.

Then Lily said, "Feldon is coming next week!"

Silence. Lily's eyes gleamed the way they did when she'd just scored big at crazy eights.

"Lily," Stan's mother said. Her eyebrows flattened. "Lily."

"It's true! Daddy told me!"

His mother twirled her fork, wound nothing on her plate.

"He called me and he told me!"

"Feldon is not coming. Your father is not coming," his mother said icily.

"He talked just to me and he said how would you like to meet your younger brother, sweetie? And I said he could stay in my room and Daddy said that would be fine!"

Silence, like after the ship has sunk and water is rushing in and you are going down and down to the bottom.

Gary got up suddenly and started stacking plates. Stan's mother hated anyone stacking plates at the table. Stan got up then too and carried away a serving dish. Soon Gary had the water running in the kitchen sink so it was hard to hear. But not impossible.

"Lily, darling," his mother said. "I want you to listen carefully. I know people in your head tell you things. That's fine. It happens to all of us." Stan went back into the dining room to pick up glasses. His mother had taken Lily onto her lap, was holding her gently.

"But he calls me!" Lily said.

She stroked Lily's hair. "I'm here, or your brother's here. We would know if your father—"

"But he gave me my own phone!"

Lily was crying, the way she always cried about her most ridiculous tales.

"I've been too indulgent with you, and I'm sorry for that. I'm sorry, Lily. You can't keep—"

"He came to my school! He—"

"Stan doesn't have a cellphone. You don't have a cellphone. We can't afford it, and your father certainly can't afford—"

"He gave me one! My own, he did! He told me not to tell you!"

Stan's mother's face was washed-out white. "If he gave you one you go upstairs right now and get it. All right?"

Lily gulped, then climbed down and clomped off. Her footsteps resounded up the stairs. Two doors slammed—her bedroom, then her closet.

Gary stood in the doorway between the kitchen and the dining room. He had tied on a red and white apron that read, *I lost my* ♥ *in Sam's Deli Disco!*

"Maybe he did give her a phone," he said.

A gaze like smoke from Stan's mother.

"She's going to be up there fiddling in her closet for the next three hours. And when I ask her, 'Lily, honey, where's the phone your father gave you?' she's going to tell me something about a rhinoceros in the park."

Gary scratched the Deli Disco part of his belly.

Welcome to the nut house, Stan thought. It's not too late to save yourself.

But Gary didn't seem to be going anywhere.

"I'm not sure where the noodle strainer goes," he said finally, before heading back into the kitchen.

6

IN THE SHADOWS near the fence from an angle slightly behind the backboard, Stan watched Gary sink a fadeaway leaner—it couldn't really be called a jump shot since he hardly got off his toes—that looked as probable as bird splatter landing straight in your eye. It hit the front rim, the backboard, whirled around twice, stopped again on the front rim, thought about falling out, then slumped back and in.

The night air was chilly. The glow from the auto-glass lights at the front of the building seemed far away.

Stan's turn. Winter is coming, he thought.

Winter is coming and there is no way I'm going to sink this shot.

He didn't even hit the rim.

"H," Gary said.

He moved like a penguin. How could he even stay upright much less bounce the ball and shoot it almost gracefully? His feet looked dainty, like Babe Ruth's rounding the bases in old newsreels, a large man tottering.

"On this one you have to be falling forward, like this, and it's a scooping shot." Gary ducked his head as if sliding under someone's outstretched arm, fell forward awkwardly and then scooped the ball underhanded way into the air—a pathetic excuse of a shot that would never work, not in a million years.

Except it did. *Swish*.

Stan bounced the ball, ducked, leaned, lost his grip, scooped with his fingertips up, up . . .

"O," Gary said.

Now he stood at the foul line—the crack where the foul line would be—with his back to the basket. The ball arced in the darkness . . . *swish!*

Stupid game, all about trick shots. Nothing to do with . . .

Janine Igwash cut through the shadows past the auto-glass sign and headed straight toward him.

"Any time tonight," Gary said.

She was watching as Stan leaned back and tried to see the basket before he flung the ball hopelessly backwards.

"R," Gary said.

"Hey," Janine said. She had a knapsack on one shoulder and she was wearing boots with heels — heels! — so she towered over him.

Stan whirled, stole the ball from Gary — *bounce bounce* — twisted in a layup, got the rebound — *bounce bounce* — sank a jumper, got the rebound, dribbled around Janine, and sank another jumper.

She wasn't looking at him like she was tilted. Whatever that might look like.

"We're playing horse," Stan puffed. He fired the ball at Gary too hard. It went through Gary's fingers. Stan chased down the ball — *bounce bounce* — then handed it back to Gary, who introduced himself to Janine and asked if she wanted to play.

"I bet you're pretty good. It's just horse. You know the rules? Stan already has H-O-R. Two more misses and he's out." He gave Janine the ball. "Just take a shot. It doesn't matter if it goes in or not. It's just a game."

Janine put her backpack down by the foul-line crack. She held the ball as if it were a vase that might explode. Weren't lesbians supposed to be good at sports? Her eyes were only for Gary. Gary! The penguin.

Janine heaved the ball in an awkward sort of set

shot, both hands pushing out. It hit the rim on the way up—way too hard!—and popped straight into the air.

And in.

Janine jumped in the air, and it was Gary who slapped her a high five and said, "Wow! You're a natural!" when she was anything but.

It was blind luck! Anyone could see!

Stan stood stiff and quiet, a human fence post.

"So now I have to make the same shot from the same place," Gary said. *Bounce bounce.* He smiled for Janine, leaned back in his improbable way, lifted himself onto his toes . . . *swish.*

"And now Stan has to make the same shot, too."

Bounce bounce. Stan felt himself flushing from his ankles to his earlobes.

This was not difficult. He could make this shot twenty times in a row on any ordinary day. *Bounce bounce.*

A jump shot is a wave that begins in the soles of the feet. It travels up through the ankles, calves, thighs, hips . . . up the spine, through the shoulder, elbow, wrist and out the fingers . . .

Clank!

"H-O-R-S!" Gary said triumphantly. Then they were at it again, Gary and Janine high-fiving.

And so it went. His mother's boyfriend and—what was Jason Biggs' stupid word? The gwog.

Stan was out in a couple more shots and then Gary missed everything after that so Janine would win.

The whole thing was some other game that Stan didn't know. Some game that made it easy for Janine to hug a middle-aged penguin but not him, not the boy she'd asked to the dance. Because it wasn't a real ask, it was all fake.

Janine shouldered her bag and slithered over the fence the same way she had the other night. But now Gary saw her, too, and it was all different.

"What a great girl!" Gary said, understanding nothing. "You'll want to hang on to her."

———

STAN'S MOTHER AND GARY went out again later that night. Stan lay still in his darkened bedroom, the ball bouncing in his head, glancing off the rim, his jump shot sputtering.

Janine's hips in Janine's jeans. Those heeled boots. She wasn't so bad with the basketball. Her hands were big. Big for a girl's. A girl whose clothes would not stay on, not entirely, not in bed with Stan in the dark while the *bounce bounce* kept bouncing . . . and parts of her moved in those boots not made for basketball, so he lay there in his usual state, his lying state . . . *in state*, like leaders lie when they're dead and stiff as a board. Were they stiff . . . all over?

How rigor did mortis get?

How pathetic was it to feel this way about a girl who was just using him?

Lily was making huffing-chuffing breathing noises in the next room.

Then she said, "Well, you have to bring Feldon!"—her voice clear in the night air.

Stan waited. Sometimes she blurted stupid things in her dreams.

"I *do* want to meet him! He's my brother!"

She went back to huffing-chuffing. She was just dreaming.

"Well, I can't hear you, either . . . I did pull up the antenna!"

Stan sat up. Blinked. Listened hard.

"I just want to see him and hug him all over," Lily said.

Stan crept out of bed. He waited by the door, listening.

Had she heard him? His lungs moved like a slow

curtain. His feet felt cold on the floor. Lily was unnaturally silent.

He took another step. Lily snuffled in her bed, rustled the blankets. In the shadows she lay on her side clutching Mr. Strawberry, pinning his shoulders to the mattress. Her eyes were shut hard.

"I know you're awake, Lily. I heard you."

Stan approached and sat lightly on the edge of her bed near her feet. Lily's lips curved in a ferocious frown. Her eyes stayed closed.

She looked like an angelic little . . .

An electronic ringtone version of "Ode to Joy" started to play somewhere within Mr. Strawberry. Lily tightened her grip on his neck but still didn't open her eyes.

"Is that a phone?"

She shoved Mr. Strawberry under her pillow and turned her back on Stan. "Ode to Joy" kept playing, slightly muffled.

"Go have a pee," Stan said. He was surprised when she simply did it—headed to the bathroom as if sleepwalking, hugging Mr. Strawberry to her chest. "Ode to Joy" went with her.

When she came back, in silence, she burrowed under the covers like an animal. Her fingers came away from Mr. Strawberry.

A minute passed, maybe two. Eventually Lily's body relaxed into regular breaths. Stan brushed a dark curl away from her eyes.

Under the Velcro flap at the back, Stan pulled out the slim phone and flipped it open. The light shone in his face.

It took a moment to figure out the menu. He pressed a few wrong buttons at first and had to backtrack. But there was the list of recent calls. All the same long-distance number.

Stan pressed something by mistake. A phone started ringing at the other end. Stan stood up and tried to see how to shut it off.

"Pumpkin, you really should be sleeping," a man's voice said. Quite deep and somehow familiar.

"Dad?" Stan said.

Then he found the button finally and turned the damn thing off.

7

THERE WERE BULRUSHES, and the sun was warm on his face. The path was muddy so he had to be careful. The bulrushes were way over his head. Blue sky past that. Nothing past the blue sky.

Where were his parents? He whacked at the bulrushes with a stick. Sometimes they exploded into clouds of little butterflies—browny white ones that flew up with the breeze over his head, not down in the heat close to the muck and the path. He whacked the stalks of the bulrushes, and when he could he jumped up with the stick and whacked the fuzzy hotdog ends where the browny white butterflies lived.

The browny white ones weren't real butterflies. They floated in the wind and sometimes he sneezed them and then it was hard to keep his sneakers out of the muck.

There would be swimming after this. Somewhere at the end of the path. He was listening for the swimming but he couldn't hear it. All he could hear was the rustle of wind through the brown dry stalks and the green wet ones. The green and the brown together made a messy wall that could open up and swallow you, so that's why he had to stay on the path.

And then his sneakers were wet, swallowed by the muck on what should have been a dry spot. First one, then the other, *squelch squelch*, and the muck smelled like toilet gas and his feet squirmed in the mucky sneakers that wanted to stay glued where they were. He nearly pulled them off just by stepping another step. So he ran and the muck got worse as the path squirmed and snaked.

Where were his parents? Where was the swimming?

So he ran and he ran and it didn't matter anymore what muck he stepped into, up to his ankles, splattering his knees.

There they were, his parents. He almost missed them! He almost ran past them hiding off the path in the green and brown wall where they'd thrown down the blanket.

He pushed through to them and said, "Where's the swimming?"

It was so hot they'd taken off some of their clothes. It was so hot down there on the blanket in the green and brown wall that Daddy and Mommy were squirming. Their underpants were at their ankles!

Stan said again, "Where is the swimming?" because his sneakers and his legs were mucky.

And Mommy turned her face to him. She looked like she'd been dreaming. Daddy had his face hiding into her neck.

"What are you doing?" Stan asked.

That's when his father lifted up his face, too. He was lying right on top of her in the hot hot and his face looked like he'd just been swimming himself.

"We're planting your little brother, Sport," he said. And Mommy hit him—it wasn't much of a slap. Her arms were mostly trapped in his.

So Stan ran to where the swimming was. It wasn't far at all and he did splash water on the sneakers and his legs till all the muck came off. Later when he looked up his parents were on the blanket on the beach in their swimsuits. His mother was reading a book and his father was sitting in his dark glasses staring at something far far away.

———

At breakfast Stan and Lily sat alone over two bowls of brown flakes. His mom and Gary were upstairs still. At least they were being quiet.

Sometimes they weren't.

"When did Dad say he was coming?" Stan pressed.

"I had a dream about kitty-cats," Lily said.

"If he's coming we really need to know," Stan said.

"There was a black one and a tawny one. Tawny is a color," she said.

"Mom, for one, is going to hit the roof."

"And that was his name, too. Tawny and Rick. They were racing and jumping off the rooftop and Rick thought he could fly." She picked up her spoon and held it, flying, over her head. Milk dripped onto the shoulder of her blouse. "And Tawny yelled out, 'Look out below!'"

Stan grabbed the spoon and put it down on the table. Lily shook her hand as if he'd hurt her.

"When is he coming?"

Lily picked up her spoon again and slurped her milk. "Rick hit the ground and died."

"How did you get that phone?"

"There was a little bounce and then his feet went splat! And there was blood where his little head—"

"Is he back in town? Did he bring it to you?"

"—bounced around like a little ball."

Stan drilled his big-brother eyes into hers until she had to look at him.

"Filled with blood," she said. "Everywhere it bounced it left a little mark."

"Lily—did he come to your school or something and bring you the phone?"

"He didn't look like any pictures. It was all gray."

"What was?"

"His beard."

"Dad has a beard?"

Lily twirled her wet spoon on the table.

"Was he waiting for you at school?"

She was a baby when their father left. What was he trying to do now? Steal her away?

"Should I tell Mommy?"

"No! Let's just keep this—"

"Because I already told her and she didn't believe me anyway. Just like you don't believe me about Rick the dead cat."

"I took the phone, Lily. If Dad's going to call anybody now, it'll be me."

———

STAN WASN'T GOING TO GO to the dance. Not with his father in town. This was high alert, code red! He had the phone in his pocket and it felt radioactive.

No way his mother would react well to his father being back. Why *was* he back? If he wasn't going to send money — he was years behind with the money — no way Mom would let him see Stan and Lily.

Why didn't he send money? Because he'd left all of them: Stan, Lily, Mom. He'd just poured gasoline on that part of his life and set it all ablaze.

Why was he phoning Lily?

Stan felt like he was standing by his locker in the middle of the storm, a storm of high-school kids whirling off in their own directions, and he was the lone calm center.

"What do you have now?" Janine Igwash said to him suddenly from only a few inches away. He didn't particularly like having to look up at her. She was in a black stretchy top that went well with the red shock of her hair and hid nothing of her form. The tattoo on the crest of her milky shoulder peeked out at him. A little lizard shaped like an S, but with legs.

"What?" He really had to work on his conversation skills.

"What class do you have now?" she said slowly and clearly, pronouncing the words through soft-looking lips.

He was not going to go to the dance with her because she was not interested in him and it was horrible to feel so stuck to the edge of his locker door by someone who wasn't even trying. She did it effortlessly by standing there.

"I don't know," he said.

"You don't know what class you have?"

The little green and red lizard rippled slightly when she breathed.

She smiled and then hooked her finger into his belt loop and tugged slightly. He fell forward, almost directly into her, into where she had been. Already she was moving off.

Heading down the hall to whatever classroom was supposed to contain her.

———

At lunchtime Stan stood outside in the cold gray air and stared at the phone. Now would be a good time for his father to call, if he was going to call. It would be a good time to have thoughts in order in case the call came, so Stan leaned back against the wall and considered.

"Dad!" he said to the cold wind. No one else was out in this wind. It was a promise-of-winter wind, a warning of cold times to come. "Why the hell are you in town?"

The phone remained mute.

Stan's father was a difficult man to figure. That much was clear, and Stan had had five years to think hard about it. His father was tall and lean and a good hockey player. Stan remembered, too, the burn of snuggling close to his cheek. He smelled . . . of aftershave or something.

He smelled like a regular father. But how was Stan to know? He'd only had the one.

Stan's father burst over things. Like Lily did, Stan thought now, except he was a lot bigger than Lily and more dangerous. Stan had a memory of spilled coffee in the kitchen—of how his father's voice cut even deeper than broken china on a bare foot.

He made you feel like everything was fine or it was all your fault. But didn't every family scream? It was all usual, right up to the moment his father left with a much younger woman and a baby on the way. Stan had never even seen a picture of them. They were phantoms, ghosts. But afterwards his father became something entirely different—a liar and a cheat and a man Stan's mother couldn't talk about anymore without the wallpaper curling from the tears and swearing.

Why was he back?

Maybe the real-estate thing he'd been pursuing—he'd quit law after running away with Kelly-Ann—had come through and now he could finally cough up the years of child support he owed.

Maybe it was over with Kelly-Ann now, too. Maybe he wanted to re-glue the family. Maybe he loved them after all. Maybe he'd spent years thinking about his kids. Maybe he was sorry.

He was. Fucking sorry. He was a sorry excuse of a father.

Stan stared at the phone.

The school door opened and Karl Brolin and his gang—Ty Blake, Nylan Leash, Jamie Hartleman—came out like a pack of dogs all barking at once and running around the lead guy. It was too cold, too windy to play, but Brolin was bouncing an old leather ball, and he headed straight to the junior hoop. He took one of his lazy falling-away jumpers—like Gary, he barely got off the tips of his toes—that clanged the rim and fell out. No wrist release. No spin on the ball. Jamie Hartleman grabbed the rebound, lobbed up a hook but Brolin palmed it above the basket. He tried for a dunk but the ball bounded off and the huge boy hung from the rim.

It was only the junior hoop—regulation height still, of course, but it was where the younger guys were allowed to play.

Now Brolin and Blake took on Leash and Hartleman. Four starters for the senior team. Leash was the only true guard. The ball was a blur when he dribbled, and he made Brolin look slow.

On one drive Leash faked a scoop shot, passed instead, but Brolin kept trying for the block . . . and Leash ended up crumpled on the pavement holding his knee.

Brolin just stood there with his hands on his hips.

"Hey! Hey, you, kid!" Hartleman yelled at Stan. "You play, don't you?"

Brolin pulled Leash to his feet, and the best point guard in the whole school hobbled around muttering obscenities at Brolin and then limped back to school.

"Don't you play?" Hartleman called.

Stan put away the phone and Hartleman snapped a bounce pass at him. The leather was slick, the ball hard to handle.

Hartleman stole the ball from Stan and dribbled around like a big crazy bug before spinning one in off the backboard. Brolin and Blake didn't even move to defend.

"I could beat you guys playing with a fire hydrant."

So Stan, the hydrant, started with the ball out near the faded three-point line. Blake didn't even bother covering him. Stan could have drilled a jumper. But the rim was bent, it was windy, and he didn't want to miss, not in front of these guys. So he passed off to Hartleman, who whirled and bobbed with the two guys on him. He glanced at Stan — wide open! — then took an off-balance left-handed hook that wasn't even close.

Thirty seconds later Brolin had a dunk and a lay-in and then Blake faked Stan out of his socks and glided free to the basket.

"Just fucking try to play," Hartleman muttered to Stan.

Down three already! Stan got lucky on a rebound Brolin was too lazy to contest and found himself concentrating on a simple shot off the backboard as if, of all the things he wanted to do in his life, this was the most important.

A point!

Twice in a row Hartleman got double-teamed and passed off to Stan for the same ten-foot jumper that rattled in despite the wind and the bent rim.

Brolin spat on the ground. They traded a couple more baskets. All tied.

Next basket wins.

Hartleman dribbled lazily beyond the three-point line. Brolin reached but missed, reached but missed. Blake went after Hartleman, too. Stan was all alone beside the basket. Hartleman bounced, bounced . . . a little whirl . . .

. . . and here was the ball finally in Stan's hands. He jumped, looked for the basket . . . .

And crumpled under the full weight of Brolin slamming him from nowhere.

"Flagrant foul!" Hartleman said. "Basket counts! Fucking basket counts!"

Everything looked very far up. The sky was gray, gray. The basket was like a bent black shadow.

"Are you like, dead, or what?" Brolin said to Stan. "My foul. Your ball. We're still tied."

The behemoth pulled him up on his feet.

Brolin placed the ball in Stan's hands, walked him to the spot behind the three-point line. Stan stood there dizzily.

Bounce, bounce. Stan's head still wasn't clear. Brolin backed off him. So Stan needed to pass it off. The thought was clear but his body wasn't responding.

"Take your best shot, kid." Brolin made a little motion with his hand. He wasn't going to defend.

Stan couldn't see where Hartleman was. He

couldn't see the basket. He could barely see Brolin, for that matter. It was all a mash . . .

But his body knew what to do. *Bounce, bounce,* a fake to the right . . . and Brolin smiled. Smiled!

Stan didn't know where the basket was till he was shooting. His wrist was releasing, and there it was finally . . . ludicrously far away.

Brolin eased into position to collect the rebound . . . which didn't come because the ball fell through pure as rain.

"In! It's in!" screamed Hartleman. Then the senior was hugging him. Screaming right in Brolin's meaty face. "We got a boy here can fucking shoot!"

The ball was blowing off toward a puddle. Blake went after it. For a moment Stan thought they'd have to play again, that Brolin was simply not going to accept the result.

But Brolin was looking at something else—at some*one*. Stan had a hard time following his gaze. He had a hard time figuring if his feet were on the ground.

But eventually he saw.

There was Coach Burgess by the door, his big hands in the pockets of his sweatpants.

8

STAN SAT THROUGH biology class trying not to stare at Janine Igwash in her clingy black top. He was trying to think of how exactly to tell her he wasn't going to the dance even though he'd said he would. But it was almost impossible because Jason Biggs, every few minutes, kept saying things like, "You and Hartleman beat Brolin and Blake two-on-two! With Burgess watching! Unbelievable!"

It *was* unbelievable. Given the wind, the bent rim, Stan's dizzy head, how far away he was when he took that shot.

He couldn't tell her about his father. That would be too much. But maybe his mother could be sick. With what? Nothing too serious. A bad flu, so Stan would have to stay home and look after Lily and it really was tough luck about the dance, thanks so much for thinking of him. He might actually be carrying flu himself so don't stand so close.

Sometimes solutions seemed to come out of the air.

"And Brolin was covering you on the last shot! That's what I heard!" Jason Biggs said. "You are *in*! You are *on* the senior team!" He shook his pimply face at the wonder of it and Mr. Stillwater looked up from his marking to glare at Stan.

They were supposed to be reading from the textbook and Stan had exactly the correct page open on his desk. But Stillwater still glared at him.

"You are *on* the senior team!" Biggs whispered again.

Tryouts wouldn't start till Monday. But Stan felt a little giddy wind inside, fluttering with the possibilities.

As soon as biology ended, Stan would walk out with Janine Igwash and tell her about his mother's flu. He'd do it in the hallway where it would be so noisy no one else would hear. "I'm so sorry," he'd say. "Maybe I shouldn't even be in class today. I might be infectious myself."

He too could be sorry.

But what was she doing inviting him in the first place?

It would be a small lie to keep other larger stupid things from happening.

"I heard Brolin was so mad he bent the junior hoop right out of shape," Jason Biggs whispered.

Stan read about how light hit the retina and created an upside-down image. *The signals intersect at the optic chiasm and cross over to the opposite side of the brain for reversal in the visual cortex.*

But what if the actual world *was* upside down and we saw clearly but our brains misprocessed all the information?

Maybe some people saw things correctly — upside down to everyone else. And maybe those same few were all in asylums banging their heads against their bedpans because everyone else was crazy.

Stan found himself flipping through the book, past cell division, past photosynthesis, past the organs of digestion . . . to the human reproductive system.

The page just fell open: *The Female Reproductive Organs.* They were fantastical shapes in yellow, pink, orange, blue. Like flowers and gourds stuck up inside shadowy female flesh. It was a brand new book so no previous student had had time to scribble foolishness on the pictures.

Stan read the bizarre labels: *Fallopian tube, Fimbriae, Follicle containing mature ovum.* And then his eyes stalled on *Clitoris: spongy, erectile, highly sensitive tissue bundled with nerve endings much like the male penis.*

The male penis. What other penis was there? Obviously this complicated little female version. Where was it? It seemed to be a blue dotted thing hidden inside the *labia minora* and *labia majora,* whatever those were.

It couldn't really be blue?

The other cross-section view didn't help, either. Here the female pelvis looked like a cow's skull split open. Stan couldn't see any legs. *Pubic symphysis.* What was that? There were the *labia minora* again, but they looked completely different from this angle. Was north up?

"Mr. Dart," Stillwater said from inches away, pinning Stan to the page like an insect in an exhibit.

Stan shut the book. Blood shot to his face.

In the gap between Stillwater's angled elbow and his predictable blue shirt, Stan could see Janine Igwash staring at him again. She had all of those things: *fallopian tubes* and a *pubic symphysis* and *labias minor* and *major.* She had a *clitoris,* somewhere.

"What are you reading?" Mr. Stillwater asked him.

Stan tried desperately to find the chapter on the

crossing of vision, whatever it was called. But every page he opened seemed to have vaginal implications.

"The eyes, sir," Stan said. "I'm reading about the eyes."

His face seemed to be giving off steam.

"The test on Monday is worth twenty percent of your term mark," Mr. Stillwater said, loud enough for everyone's benefit. "I'm not going to ask you any-thing about—" and he paused for effect — "female reproduction, or menstruation, or the male and female sexual response."

Explosions of hilarity, which set perspiration streaming from Stan's pits to his belly and down his legs. Even sitting, he seemed to be naked in the shower in front of them all.

He could not look at Janine.

No way he could tell her after this.

Mr. Stillwater was playing it like a stand-up comedian. But it couldn't last forever.

He was done in maybe a minute at most.

The rest of the class took forever.

———

AT THE END OF THE DAY she was standing on the sidewalk in her clingy black top despite the cool wind. From the front door he could see her nipples straining against the fabric. She was standing all alone, not looking at anything in particular. As far as he could tell she was just silently . . . attracting him.

He felt himself pulled out to where she stood. The closer he got, the stronger her powers.

"Stillwater has some kind of thing for you," she said.

He was ready with his own opening remarks, but they fled as his face turned into a furnace again. He stood far enough away that she couldn't just reach in and tug his belt loop.

She was absolutely beautiful.

"I thought . . . I thought I should tell you something before we go tomorrow," she said.

He cut her off. "I was going to say something about . . . my mother." It was self-preservation. She was about to tell him about her preferences, because she was a decent person after all.

"Your mother?"

"Yeah, my mom is . . . uh . . . sick."

"Really?"

It felt like someone had fired a staple into the back of his throat. He could lie to this girl but it wasn't easy.

He coughed and tried to swirl some spit in his mouth to dislodge whatever was clawing back there.

"Because that's what *I* was going to say to *you*," she said. "My mom has cancer. She's been through everything—chemo, radiation. She had the surgery. She just looks a little odd. When you meet her. But she's fine. I mean, she's not fine. But she's just a person, too."

Stan could barely swallow. The staple had closed down nearly everything.

"You know how survivors are. That's all I'm saying. She comes on pretty strong sometimes. Are you all right?"

Stan bent over and coughed. He didn't want to spit in front of her but he couldn't see any way around it. He turned away from the wind and did what he had to do to clear his throat.

"Fine," he croaked.

"What's *your* mother dealing with?" Janine asked.

"She's, uh . . . she's romantically obsessed," Stan said, surprising even himself.

"Is that an illness?" Janine's teeth beamed at him. Stan remembered his father telling him once—years ago, of course—to be careful of a girl's teeth. It had been an odd thing to say at the time and now he wondered about it.

He was only inches away from kissing her. How did he end up only inches away? And how did one go about kissing, anyway? What was the protocol? In movies the guy always seemed to know when to do it. Or the girl jumped the guy and they kissed.

Janine looked like she might be about to jump him. Stan braced himself.

"Romantic obsession?" she said again. "Is that an illness?"

"It is with my mom," Stan said. And then suddenly the staple was gone. "My mom and dad are divorced." He pulled out the phone. "But Dad is back in town now. I keep expecting him to call any minute. It's all a big secret. He had a kid with somebody else. And he's not supposed to be here and he hasn't paid us any support in, like, forever. But he gave this phone to my sister and . . ."

Why was he telling her all this? He'd never told anybody.

"I'm sorry about your mother," he mumbled.

Janine didn't blink. "She's amazing, really. She might still live way past what we think. When was the last time you saw your father?"

Stan was about to say, "Five years ago." But a flash of something caught his eye—a gray beard on a man who was leaning against the wall of the coffee shop across the street, staring at him.

Was that his father?

Stan honestly couldn't tell. This man looked stockier than his dad, shorter—but of course men gained weight, especially in middle age, and Stan had grown taller over the past few years. The beard was full and hid the man's face.

Was that his father?

Janine's hand just casually touched his. Stan's senses sprang into high alert. A girl was wrapping her fingers around his!

"Are you all right?" she said.

The man—his father?—was gone. Slipped into the coffee shop, maybe.

"I don't see anybody," Janine said.

"My family got hit by a crazy bomb five years ago, and nobody's been anywhere near sane since," Stan said. "That's what I want to tell you before tomorrow. Just to give you fair warning."

"Does that mean you don't want to go?"

Her fingers were interlaced with his now. How did that happen? One little tug from either of them—just the way she'd pulled on his belt loop before—and they'd be kissing. Right here on the open sidewalk in front of the whole world.

In front of his father, maybe, who'd probably stepped into the coffee shop and was looking at them through the darkened window.

"Did I tell you I'm a terrible dancer?" Stan said.

She was not looking away. She just kept standing there looking highly kissable.

"I can't dance, either," she said.

He laughed. She moved like—Stan didn't know what. Like a river. Like a sleek, tawny animal slipping through the brush.

Tawny. Lily's word gave him the strength to unlace his fingers and step away.

"Maybe we both should wear steel-toed boots," he said. Then his legs were taking him off, off to safety.

9

STAN WASN'T HOME A minute before his mother ordered him into the car.

"It's the appointment!" she said. "With the principal. For Lily!"

"That's now?" he said.

"It's in six fucking minutes!" she said. "Sorry for my language. Don't you ever swear like me." He could see her jaw was nearly locked. There was no point asking her why she hadn't told him until just now.

Stan's mother got in the car and fumbled with the ignition key, her hands shaking.

It wasn't just Lily. What else had happened?

"Do you want me to drive?" Stan asked.

"Drive? *You?*" Stupid of him to even mention it. His mother was in a state. She had to be almost Zen calm to drive with him.

She was never Zen calm.

"Forget it," he said. He settled back in his seat beside her. She swore again under her breath and crumpled against the steering wheel.

"I suppose you should," she said.

"No, no, it's all right!"

Too late. She opened the door and jerked herself out.

"You're sixteen, you need to learn these things. I can't keep holding you back!"

Stan slid over awkwardly. His mother jolted into the passenger seat.

"If I were a better parent I'd be taking you out driving every night." She thrust over the keys.

"Mom."

"If I were a better parent you'd be in driver's ed. You'd have your license by now."

"You're a great parent, Mom."

"Shut up. Do up your seatbelt!"

If he could drive with his mother, Stan thought, he could drive with anybody. He clicked his belt, adjusted the mirrors, flicked the lights on and off.

"What was that for?"

"Just testing." Stan switched on the left turn signal, and the wipers.

"For God's sake, Stanley! We're already late!"

It had been so long since his last practice session he'd forgotten what all the controls were. That's all. He pressed down the clutch with his left foot.

It was all in the balance. As the clutch came out, the gas went down.

He wiggled the stick shift. Reverse was toward him, down the slot.

"Any time this afternoon, Stanley," his mother breathed.

He turned the key and the engine coughed to life. This was all going to be fine. Lots of idiots learned how to drive. Stan pulled the stick into reverse. He let up on the clutch. Don't rocket out. Don't—

The car lurched back, then stalled.

"All right!" his mother said, undoing her seatbelt. "This isn't the time for a lesson."

"I can do it! Honest!"

"You're going to kill the car!"

Stan stayed quiet, didn't move. She did up her belt again.

"Just take it easy . . ."

Stan had drained the winning shot against Karl Brolin in a high wind on a bent rim from too far away. He could do this, too. It was all about balance. Clutch and gas. Release one, press the other . . . and the car reversed down the driveway as smooth as butter.

He was doing it!

"Which way should I signal if I'm backing left, but going right?" he asked calmly.

"Nobody signals going backwards! Look out!"

A woman with a stroller was half a block down the road and going in the opposite direction.

Stan didn't bother signaling. Technically, he knew he was supposed to signal. He remembered that at least from the driving regulation book he'd spent some time with months ago. It was the balance that was important. Clutch went in, gas went out . . . gas in, clutch out. How many times did people tell him? But until you actually knew it in your body . . .

"We can't take forever!" his mother nearly shouted. Stan shifted into first, then proceeded down the street. He left ample room for the woman and stroller. Second was easy.

"I'm going the speed limit," Stan said. It was hard not to keep his voice a deadpan in reaction to his mother's rising anxiety. But inside, trumpets were blowing.

He was driving the stick shift!

"You're close to the ditch!"

Stan eased over slightly. His mother wasn't used to sitting in the passenger seat. Everything looked close to the ditch from there.

"Do we know what Lily has done this time?" Stan asked. He turned onto Broadlane, shifting gears like a professional, and stayed beautifully in sync with the traffic. It was Friday rush hour. Worst time to be driving. But they didn't have far to go.

"The principal wouldn't say anything on the phone," Stan's mother said. *"Honey—!"*

A boy on a bicycle wobbled on the sidewalk nowhere near where they were. Even if he fell he was too—

Stan braked, a little harshly, for the light, and the engine bucked and his mother lurched forward and was caught, roughly, by her seatbelt. She glared at him.

But it was all right. No damage. Everything started again. He liked the feel of the vehicle. He liked pressing ahead smoothly, that harmony between left foot and right, and the way the car took a turn and how the steering wheel spun back more or less by itself as the road straightened. He could feel it now in his body. In a couple of months he was going to be a better driver than his mother.

Well, maybe that wouldn't be so hard.

He had another thought that seemed profound: *the car wants to stay on track.*

If you stayed between the lines you eventually got to where you were going.

Which was Lily's school.

When Stan parked finally—perfectly between the yellow markers—his mother's face was deathly white.

———

THE NEW PRINCIPAL, Ms. Shorey, looked too young to be sitting where she was sitting.

She did not seem ready to send Lily to remedial classes. In fact, Lily was sitting in the principal's office, too, and her face was lit with some new kind of fire. She and the principal had obviously been talking quite a bit in the last while.

But Stan's mother started in anyway.

"I know what you're going to say and I'm really sorry. Things have not been as settled at home as I would like and so it's hard to spend as much time with Lily as I really need to. Stanley does his best with her but he's busy in high school. Normally I'm there to supervise and to keep her focused . . ." The principal was looking at Stan's mother oddly. "She can be a real handful sometimes as I'm sure you know!"

Ms. Shorey beamed for a moment at Lily. "The results of the comprehensive cognitive testing came in today." She shuffled some papers and put them back down on her desk.

"Oh, God, not more tests," Stan's mother muttered.

"Lily has scored exceptionally high in particular aptitudes," Ms. Shorey said. She could not seem to contain herself. "In all my years in education I have never—"

"I'm sorry," Stan's mother broke in. "Aptitudes?" The word did not seem to go with "Lily."

"Lily is not only above average in imaginative actualization," the principal said. "She's stratospheric."

What was the word for her smile?

Toothpastey.

"But her math, her reading—I mean, this girl has never had a strong report card in her life!" Stan's mother said. Lily turned a sour look on her. "I'm sorry, sweetie, but you haven't."

"All those conventional scores have probably been suppressed by Lily's imaginative capabilities," Ms. Shorey said. "She is light years beyond what most children—" Lily nodded slightly, like a princess receiving a tiara.

"Her head is in the clouds," Stan's mother said.

"In the most refreshing ways," Ms. Shorey continued. Stan's mother blew through her pressed lips, *pffft*.

"At any rate," the principal persisted, "what I'm trying to do today is open a dialogue with you about possibilities for Lily's future. As you know the regular school system is not geared for children with exceptional abilities . . ."

Stan could almost hear the sequence of thoughts clicking over in his mother's mind: there was no extra money for any special education program; no extra money for anything, actually; Lily was going to have to fit in with the regular kids.

"So I'm thinking about putting Lily's name forward for Gifted Exceptions. She'll have to submit to more testing, of course, and you'd have to agree."

"Gifted Exceptions?" Stan's mother was on the edge of her seat, nearly standing. "I'm afraid we—"

"We don't run the program here. But it is part of the regular school system. Completely funded. I wrote about it in the opening week newsletter." Ms. Shorey looked almost hurt that someone had failed to read her article.

But it was the word "funded" that worked its magic on Stan's mother. She eased slightly back into her chair.

"You're telling me that Lily has above-normal intelligence in—"

"Intuitive actualization. She creates whole worlds, other parallel realities, and peoples them at the same time that she functions in the so-called normal modes of reality. I was completely the same way when I was young. I recognized it in Lily as soon as we started chatting. She's an *exceptional* child."

Lily quivered. Stan tried to remember the last time she'd stayed this quiet this long.

"My Lily is . . ."

"An exceptionally gifted child. And there's a program for her at Barclay Heights school. It's a farther bus ride away . . ."

Lily nodded lightly in time with the rhythm of the words, like she had composed them herself and was now hearing them in someone else's song.

———

ON THE RIDE HOME Lily gazed, beamingly, out the window. Stan could just see the edge of her face in the rearview mirror.

The car nearly drove itself. It really wasn't that difficult to stay in line, to follow the signs and the lights, turn the wheel and press the pedals and get from A to B.

Stan's mother seemed distracted. Was it more than

this situation with Lily? Maybe it had to do with the governance committee at work. Stan had no idea what such a committee did. They governed something, perhaps, and at times she talked about it a lot.

Stan's mother had worked in the same office for years. She was pretty high up by now, but she wasn't running the place.

It was hard to imagine his mother running anything.

"How was work today, Mom?" Stan asked. "Everything all right with the . . . governance committee?"

No reaction. Did she even hear?

Lily started humming. She didn't like people talking about things that didn't concern her.

"The governance committee has got its head up its ass," Stan's mother said finally. "I've stopped worrying about the governance committee." She let out a long stream of breath through taut lips.

Stan could remember when she used to smoke. He was very small then and she would hug him fiercely and blow the smoke over his head. He remembered the sting of it in his eyes and nose.

"We did get an unusual memo today from head office," she said then. "All nonessential travel has been canceled. There's a general staff meeting called for 9:15 Monday morning. With a video link-up, too . . . *Stanley!*"

It was nothing. Two children crossing the road on the yellow. He wasn't planning on running the light anyway.

It was all under control.

"So you think the place is—"

"Shaky. The accountants have been walking around not looking anybody in the eye for weeks now. Of course, the downturn has meant that funders are far less likely to . . ."

Stan's mother's organization, New Page, sent books to disadvantaged countries all over the world. This much Stan knew. Most of the books were donated, but they still had to be shipped and there still had to be a partner at the other end to make sure they got to waiting schools and libraries. Languages had to be coordinated. The books had to be collected, sorted, evaluated, catalogued and warehoused before they were sent.

It all took a lot of organization. Somehow this crazy woman beside him kept herself together during the work day to do her part.

"It's not, like, bankruptcy, is it?" Stan asked. He was just driving now, his hands and his feet controlling the car. He was driving and talking at the same time. He had a vague idea that nonprofits couldn't go bankrupt, but he wasn't sure.

"I don't know what it is," she said.

They were almost home. A couple more blocks.

Lily suddenly stopped humming and said, "Dad is coming for dinner, okay?"

Stan's mother slammed her foot against the floor. If she'd been driving she would have set off the airbag.

"Lily, don't tell such lies!"

"It's not a lie. He's coming! He's coming!" She made an angry song of it and twisted in her seat in time with the words.

"I don't care what your principal calls you. Don't lie, young lady! You know the difference between truth and lies."

"He's coming! I saw him!"

"If you can't show me that you have at least one foot in this reality there's no way I will ever let you go to that special school. Do you understand?"

Stan didn't hear Lily's reply. He was distracted by something—someone—sitting on the front porch. Stan had to concentrate to glide the car up the narrow driveway. All he saw, at first, was a flash of gray.

Then he parked and they could all look at the strangely bearded man sitting on the steps as if he'd forgotten his keys.

"Daddy!" Lily squealed, and she was out of the car and squirming in his arms.

10

IT WASN'T STAN'S FATHER. Couldn't be. For one thing, Stan's father was taller than this mopey man. He was tall and angular and athletic. Stan's father used to skate right past all defenders—two, three quick strides—and cut around the net with his long reach and tuck the puck inside the post before anyone even knew what had happened.

Stan's father could whip a baseball the length of the driveway and curve it so wickedly you had to watch the spin on the seams to have any chance of knowing what the ball might do. And if you missed it you'd have to run all the way through the backyard and under the hedge and into the Farquardsons' garden to get it.

Stan's father could pick up a kid and twirl him like a helicopter blade so fast you were almost flying.

This man—this imposter—had to straighten himself up just to avoid looking Stan in the eye. He had soft shoulders and a paunch and weak eyes, saggy in the corners. Not the dark, glinting ping-pong champion beamers that Stan remembered.

He looked like a man who'd abandoned his kids years ago.

"Ron," Stan's mother said.

"Isabelle," Ron said.

They stood on the little walkway in front of the house. Lily was still draped all over him. He pressed her thick hair to his neck as if hanging on to a cliff-face vine.

All right, his father would do that. But this man—Ron—was crumbling in the corners. He looked like all the other middle-aged men Stan's mother had dated in the past few years.

"What are you doing here?" Stan's mother asked.

Ron buried his pudgy hand in Lily's hair and mumbled something about bus fare.

"What's bus fare got to do with anything?"

"There was a special on. I saw a flyer for it and so I thought I'd come."

Ron still hadn't looked Stan square in the eye. Stan might as well have been a fence post. It was up to his father to say something.

Up to Ron, who wasn't up to much.

"That wasn't our agreement," Stan's mother said. "You can't come here and disrupt everything just because there's a special on."

"I'm special," Lily blurted. "I'm going to go to a special school!"

"Please get down, Lily," her mother said.

"Why can't we just have a visit?" Ron pleaded.

"They tested me and I'm extraordinary," Lily said, not getting down. Ron gripped her tighter.

This man made Gary look good.

"I just hopped on a bus. That's all—"

"You just owe us four years, three months' worth of child support!" Stan's mother turned her icy gaze on Lily. "*Lily.*"

Lily hugged the man—Ron—all the harder. Stan imagined taking out the side of his knee with a sweeping kick. He'd collapse like a broken tent pole.

"Look, I'm not here to make any trouble," Ron said. He put Lily down. She clung still, a koala bear grappled to a tree limb. Ron squatted and blew a quick puff to clear the hair from her eyes.

That was something his father used to do.

"Did you bring your checkbook?" Stan's mother said. "Or I'd be happy to take cash." Then, because she couldn't help herself, she said again, "*Lily.*"

Lily didn't move.

If Stan had his broom handle he could sidekick the innocent grin off Ron's face.

"Look. This wasn't meant to be a big thing. I just saw the ad—"

"What are you doing for work these days, Ron?" Stan's mother asked.

Ron laughed bitterly. "That's what it always comes down to with you. What's the bottom line? What's the measure of a man's worth?"

Stan's mother's chest shivered with quick little phony breaths. Either she was going to faint from lack of air or claw his eyes out.

"I'm a carpenter," Ron said finally. He opened his hands—his pudgy, white, non-callused hands.

"From law to real estate to carpentry," she snapped.

Then a miserable gaze between the two. Stan fell into the trap of it for a time. It was hard to look away. But finally he stepped in and took Lily's wrist—not harshly, not softly—and pulled her into the house.

"He's not going to stay," she whined in the vestibule. Stan wanted to wait close enough so he could spring to his mother's aid if need be.

"He doesn't deserve to," Stan said.

He couldn't make out what they were saying out there.

They weren't screaming. That was something.

Carpentry? Stan remembered his father trying to replace a spoke on Stan's bicycle years and years ago. He remembered the wrenches, the sweat, the swear words rising to the basement rafters. And the new spoke broken, poking through the replacement inner tube. The blood on Stan's father's knuckles.

Carpentry.

Stan's mother came through the door. Stan glimpsed the front walk. Ron was gone. He'd left on foot for somewhere.

"The end of a bloody marvelous day," she said and closed the door by leaning all of her weight against it.

———

STAN MADE DINNER. Pancakes, his one dish. The recipe was in a beat-up old family cookbook with stained and smelly pages. They were low on fresh milk so he used powdered, which they were also low on. Stan's mother usually did the weekly grocery shopping Saturday morning, so often Friday dinner was sparse.

Flour was in short supply, too, so he used more baking powder than usual and slipped in extra sugar to keep Lily happy.

Not too much of the batter splashed on the stovetop. And there was bacon—last week's, still hanging tough.

If she'd just give him the money he'd do the shopping and they wouldn't run out like this.

Stan's mother wandered the house glued to Gary through her telephone.

"Well, what am I supposed to do? . . . I didn't! I didn't invite him! . . . I suppose somehow he's been in contact with Lily. Despite our agreement! Why the hell would I be surprised by anything he does at this point?"

Ron's phone was still in Stan's backpack. But if he told her . . .

Now was not the time.

There was no oil so the pancakes didn't stick together particularly well. They burned to the nonstick pan instead. The smoke alarm was going to go off any minute.

Water-paste pancakes, charred and crumbling. At least there was syrup. Lily might eat them yet.

"He told me that Kelly-Ann and Feldon have gone to stay with her uncle . . . She's in pre-law. He's got money to pay for that. Maybe they're still using her family money. And he's a fucking carpenter."

She was in her work outfit still, her blouse and pressed pants, but with the sorry yellow knitted slippers she tended to wear around the house. Little pompoms bounced when she thudded across the floor.

"I don't know if she kicked him out or not!"

The smoke alarm sounded then. Not the family-room alarm, which was closest, but the upstairs-landing alarm. Stan called out to Lily to whack it with the broom.

"You're going to have to do it yourself," Stan's mother said.

He only had batter left for another few pancakes. *"Lily!"*

"It's a madhouse here," his mother said into the phone.

Stan charged up the stairs and swatted the alarm off the ceiling. It howled on the floor until he pried it open with his fingers and released the battery into silence.

———

LATER, WHEN THE BLACKENED remains of dinner had been cleared away, the three of them, the rump of a family, watched a dating show on television in which former celebrities tried to give romantic advice to contestants whose prize was to end up with each other in full public view. Even Lily stayed quiet, hypnotized by the quick cuts, the glitzy narration, the thunderous commercials. Here was a troubled young woman lying on her bed in semi-darkness—without pants, for some reason, the whites of her legs glimmering—moaning about how easily she'd shed her clothes, and was she too inviting, and would he ever call the number she had made sure he had?

"The weirded-out thing is," she said, "like, do I even like this guy? Is it, like, too late to be asking?"

She was wearing bangley earrings and her lips seemed puffed out. Nothing about her was attractive except . . .

. . . except Stan felt himself possessed of a ridgepole for no good reason whatsoever.

Sitting on the sofa with his mother and his sister as this young woman in her underwear moved her legs.

Where was the blanket? On the back of the sofa.

The young woman said, "Sometimes I just really want to jump a guy and I have no idea why."

Stan twisted to retrieve the blanket, trying hard not to press—anything—against anybody.

"What's wrong?" his mother said. Waking up from some thought.

The young woman wiggled her butt and said, "There's nothing wrong with, like, healthy sexuality. But I really should be able to remember his last name."

Stan settled the blanket on his lap. The young woman disappeared, replaced by a ripped guy pumping weights in the gym who said, "She let me in, why wouldn't I?"

"Lily, I don't think you should be watching this," his mother said. She picked up the remote and pressed a button. Nothing happened.

"Why not? Why can't I?" Lily howled.

"Stanley? Stanley, can you fix this?"

Stan took the remote. The veins in his head throbbed as he skipped through from show to show.

Lily hit him with the pillow.

"But I want to see it!" The blanket shifted and Stan pulled it back.

He stayed exactly where he was, waiting for the bubble of the evening to settle somewhere and die.

———

IN THE MIDDLE OF THE NIGHT, long after he'd gone to bed but failed to sleep, Stan sat on the front porch in the chilly air, his feet near freezing, bare on the wood. He fingered his father's phone.

It glowed in chill darkness. He hit the buttons.

"Hello?" came a voice at last. "Lily? Is that you?"

"Hi, Ron." Stan shocked himself addressing his father that way, and yet—why not?

"Oh," Ron said.

Breathing on the other end. The street lamps, everything, so still.

"It was good to see you today, son," Ron said. "I'm sorry to surprise you like that. I just saw the . . . ad, for the bus fares—"

"Does it get any better?" Stan blurted. Was that his question?

More breathing at the other end of the line. Stan thought he could hear noises in the background. At the bus station? Was it open this time of night?

What time was it?

"Does what get any better?" Ron asked.

"Getting an erection for some girl on TV," Stan said. "Thinking about it all the time. Sitting at the table at breakfast over cereal and being hard as a poker in your pajamas over nothing. Nothing!"

Not a word. If anybody knew about this, it would be his father.

"What are you talking about, Stan?"

Off. Off with the phone.

———

STAN SMELLED SMOKE on his way up the stairs and back to bed. He remembered that he hadn't replaced the battery in the smoke alarm from the burnt pancake episode, but this wasn't house-fire smoke. It was coming from a cigarette.

From the back porch, in fact. The smell grew sharper as Stan crept back through the kitchen. In the years since his mother had quit he'd grown more sensitive, so that now the smoke from a single cigarette seemed to fill the whole house.

His mother was smoking again. She was on the back porch in the dark, her head resting against the screened window, the orange bead of the cigarette perched in mid-air. Her hair was loose and long and looked as though she'd been bunching it in her hands.

He watched her from the open doorway. She was letting the cold into the house, letting in the smoke. He'd grown up with it but Lily hadn't. Somehow it seemed to him that Lily ought to be protected from the dangers.

He stood by the open door. It would be the easiest thing in the world to turn around, slip back up the stairs. He could make sure Lily's door was shut against the cancer.

Janine's mother had cancer. He'd be meeting her tomorrow night. Tonight, actually, since today had morphed into Saturday.

Stan stared at the orange bead, at his mother in shadows gazing into the backyard where the winter's chill was already in the air even though that season was technically still a few months away. He could feel it on his face, in his feet.

Surely she knew he was there? She used to know every thought in his head, every hand snaking into the cookie jar. Every nightmare.

She was wrapped in her old brown robe, and her feet were tucked up beneath her.

Stan heard himself say, "I sank a shot against Karl Brolin today in the wind on a bent rim way too far to even try it."

She didn't startle or drop the lengthening ash on the cigarette. Stan wished she'd put it out. But she just turned her head and smiled a little bit.

It was the middle of the night. They might have been in a dream. But everything felt normal somehow.

"Who's Karl Brolin?"

Stan went out and sat on the wicker loveseat opposite her and pulled a blanket around himself. It smelled of the damp, of outdoors. He told her about the whole improbable basketball game and she listened, in her way. Tossing a ball into a hoop was as unlikely an event for her as knitting this blanket would have been for him. (Was it even knitted? Crocheted? What was the difference?)

And then somehow he was telling her about Janine Igwash. He told her about the belt loop, about the invitation to the dance. About Janine's mother.

"Breast cancer?" his mother said.

The cigarette was out now, squashed into a little plate she must have brought out. There were no ashtrays left in the house. She must have a pack, but Stan couldn't see it anywhere. Only one stub and its ashes littered the plate.

Silence strung between them like the smoke. Stan rubbed his cold toes and waited.

"I had a boyfriend once whose mother had cancer," she said finally.

"Really?"

It was the middle of the night and the normal rules of disengagement seemed suspended. He wanted to hear about that boyfriend.

"I was in university and he was a sergeant, I think."

"What, a cop?" Stan said. His mother practically broke out in a rash whenever she saw policemen in the street.

"No, in the military."

His mother, the pacifist, with a soldier? His mother who wanted all arms banned from—

"He was staring at me in a store. A liquor store. I was just old enough to buy my own booze and there was this older man—he was probably all of twenty-seven—with the darkest eyes. He looked like Omar Sharif. He wasn't in uniform or anything. But you know a military man. You can see it in the way he holds himself. In his haircut, too, of course. But—"

"What was his name?" Stan felt like he was learning more about his mother in just a few minutes on this freezing back porch than in his whole life so far.

"I think it was Pete."

"You *think*?"

She was talking about some guy she used to love—some guy she probably had sex with and still thought of all these years later—and she didn't even remember his name?

"He stared at me across the wine rack. His eyes just . . . stared. Maybe I smiled at him. My face went baking scarlet. I remember that. Then when I was at the checkout he was right behind me. He smelled . . . like an animal. Like he wanted to bend me over the counter right there."

It helped, maybe, that Stan could barely see her. He could feel her looking straight at him. This might be a dream.

"So what did you do?"

"Tuesdays, after sociology and before dinner at the dorm, I met him at his friend's apartment about a twenty-minute walk from campus. The apartment hadn't been cleaned in months and I was never sure about the sheets. Often we didn't bother with sheets. He lived on base. I forget how he could get off for fifty-five minutes on Tuesday afternoons."

"Fifty-five minutes?"

"Everything was precise. Except when the clothes came off." She hesitated, and Stan could see that she'd been drinking wine, that most of the bottle on the table by the window was empty. She wasn't drunk, but maybe she wouldn't remember any of this in the morning?

"When his clothes came off he was more like a dancer. A really good dancer, as much an animal as an artist. His body . . ." She sighed, blew out as if she were still smoking. "We should all get to love a body like that at least once in our lives."

"Weren't you in university when you met Dad?" Stan asked. The question just slipped out, a product of the darkness, the hour. When she hesitated again—when she looked at him finally with her sad, sad eyes—he wished he could have taken the question back, reeled it out of the night air.

"It felt like . . . Tuesday afternoons, for fifty-five minutes, I got to be somebody else entirely. I didn't have to talk. I didn't have to wash. I didn't have to . . . follow any of the natural laws of the universe. There was only . . . the law of desire. Everything else . . ."

The night seemed to have quietly drained her store of words.

"I would carry the taste of him," she said finally. "On my body, in my clothes, on the edges of my fingers, for hours afterwards."

She looked at Stan then, as if suddenly aware of what she was saying, of who they both were.

She had a Tuesday-afternoon lover the same time she was with the guy who was going to be her husband.

"You said his mother had cancer," Stan said quickly.

"She was dying of it. I never met her." She leaned forward—a small almost-ready-to-go movement. "I think maybe Tuesday afternoons he visited her before getting to me. And that's why he was so . . . hungry. I never felt entirely as if he wanted me so much as life. He was . . . starving for life . . ."

She stood then but had to lean against the porch frame.

"My leg's fallen asleep," she said, the wine glass in her hand.

She wasn't leaving yet.

"I wish I knew what to say to you. You are such a beautiful boy. So beautiful." She ran a hand through his hair as if it were hers — bunch and release, bunch and release. "Be careful with this girl. Everything is in hot coals right now for her. Her feelings, her reactions. She's going to . . ."

Stan's mother stopped messing with his hair. She tipped her glass to sip the last few drops.

"Actually, I don't know what the hell she's going to do," she said. "I have no idea what anybody's going to do. Your father showing up today . . . he really rattled me. I didn't think he could anymore. But he wants something. He's not telling us the whole story, not by a long shot. He wants something and I don't know what it is."

His mother shook her head wearily.

"Years from now," she said, "when you're in therapy trying to sort out your life, and you're cursing me and your father for what we did or didn't do . . ." She put her face in her hands. "Oh, Jesus."

"What?"

"I know I'm a rotten mother. But I have tried to protect you from the worst of the shit. And at least I'm not a liar. I haven't told you the half of it, and I won't. But whenever you're dealing with your father, just remember. You can only trust a sliver of what the man says."

She hugged him hard in the dull light.

"And I don't believe I'm just being bitter when I say that."

11

Stan had a memory of driving with his father. When was that? Some years before it all fell apart and Ron left for Kelly-Ann and his new life. They were in their old van, back when it seemed that every family had a van. Stan used to sit behind the dashboard on the passenger's side pretending he was in the cockpit of an airplane.

That van had throat problems. It rattled even when it sat in the driveway.

And Stan's father had a smell that day. Was he drinking? He smelled dangerous, somehow. Stan remembered watching his father's hands on the wheel. It must have been a Saturday. His father wasn't at the office. Stan wasn't at school.

They were driving somewhere Stan had never been before, down to the river in an unusual part of town to go fishing. Stan's father seemed jagged and sharp around the edges, like a piece of glass your hand finds in the water when you're reaching for something else.

Did they say anything?

Finally they were there. It was sunny, not early morning by any means—when the fish had their breakfast—but maybe they would catch something. They walked together across a park and down to the public dock that jutted out over brownish water. It smelled vaguely oily, and the sunlight only penetrated the first few inches.

"If you cast over that way," his father said, pointing stiffly to a spot beyond the reeds, "I think you might get some bass."

A strange thought now popped into Stan's head: that his father had spent the entire car ride rehearsing this brief speech.

"Did you go fishing here before?" Stan asked.

Where was Lily in this memory? She must have been very small. Maybe she was home with his mother.

Stan's father didn't answer the question. He set up Stan's line with a bobber, with a hook and a rubber worm.

"See if you can hit that spot," he said. "Do you want to try my rod?"

It was a big one with a spin-caster reel. Stan did want to try it.

It took a couple of efforts. He wasn't used to releasing the line with his finger at just the right instant. But on the third or fourth cast, the bobber splashed somewhere near the quiet, deep spot his father had pointed out.

"That's it. That's good!" his father said.

They had brought two rods, but the second rod—Stan's little one—stayed on the dock.

"I'm going to be meeting . . . an associate," his father said. Associate sounded like someone important. Like someone a lawyer might have to meet on a Saturday morning instead of fishing with his boy.

Was Stan really recalling this properly? He remembered the word associate, and then his father was gone—disappeared somewhere into the neighborhood across the park.

The bobber bobbed and the minutes slowed. Two rods but one fisherman. A man was painting fence posts near the road—not the red fence itself but the posts, which were white and thick and high.

Stan reeled in slowly, then recast. He was getting better at hitting the spot. The bass must have wondered about so many rubber worms splashing overhead with red and white bobbers attached to them. The fence was red and white. So were the bobbers, so was the fishing box.

Stan didn't have a watch. Where was the sun? He couldn't remember where it had been when he started. But the fence posts were slow work. Maybe fifteen minutes a post? And the man had done two and a half already.

More than half an hour.

When the man had finished eleven and a half posts, when the fence was almost finished, Stan felt a huge tug on the line and he dropped the rod, then nearly kicked it into the water in panic. When he recovered, the line felt heavy, as if he might be pulling some monster from the deep.

A black waterlogged branch floated reluctantly to the surface. But half the rubber worm was gone, bitten off by something exciting, Stan thought. If you looked closely at the remaining portion of the rubber worm, you could see the teeth marks of the vicious fish.

At thirteen posts the fence was done. Stan climbed a willow tree, sat in the shade over the water and held his stomach where he was getting hungry.

The van was still there. But maybe the associate was a murderer? Maybe his father's body was in the basement of one of those houses by the park by the river. Maybe . . .

Maybe if he just waited a little longer, everything was going to be all right.

12

SATURDAY MORNING WAS for chores. It was a routine established by Stan's father long ago, one of the few things that had survived the separation catastrophe.

Stan tidied, dusted and vacuumed the living room, the front hallway, the kitchen, the stairs, landing and his own bedroom. His mother handled both bathrooms, the laundry and her room. Lily dawdled and played in the den and in her own room, turned on the vacuum for some seconds and, when yelled at, straightened up a few things, then collapsed in exhaustion while Stan wiped a layer of dust from the television and straightened the pictures on top of the piano that no one played.

Stan had taken precisely two lessons, at gunpoint practically, and then was not forced to continue after Other Events intervened.

Stan remembered his mother pulling down the curtains for some reason—lurching in a screaming rage and pulling them off the rod. What was that about? They were white with wavy stripes, and she had sent Ron out to get them and he'd taken all day. So he must have been with Kelly-Ann, and that must have been the day his mother found out and that was why she was pulling the curtains down and shrieking like a wounded animal.

Where did these memories hide year after year? Why were they spooling out now?

Stan gathered up the week's mostly unread newspapers and took them downstairs to the recycle box.

Maybe his mother should have sold the house when Ron moved out. They should have started fresh somewhere. Because everything here had a memory still tied to the catastrophe.

There was his father's workbench, where he used to putter for hours in the gloom away from everybody. What did he do down here? He sanded things, and hammered and cut other things, and arranged his tools on their special hooks. How could he be so quiet and patient working on his own projects and turn into such a swearing wreck out in the light of day? Stan remembered him fighting with the downspout when it came loose from the side of the house after some rainstorm. He was trying to fit a new piece, but the jagged edges of the aluminum cut at his hands like an enemy.

Did he lose it just because Stan was watching? Where was his mother in that scene? Had they just fought?

How could this bleeding, angry klutz now make a living as a carpenter?

The phone rang mid-morning.

"Hey," Janine said. "There's something else I need to tell you about tonight."

Stan waited. He was leaning against the stove trying to have a private conversation on the last phone in the world that was connected to the wall by a cord, and Lily was banging on the piano in the den instead of cleaning it.

"You really aren't very good on the phone," she said.

Clank, clank, bang, crash, crash went the piano.

"That's my little sister," Stan said. "She's teaching herself to become Mozart."

"Is she?" Janine said. "I really can't tell if you're kidding."

Stan held the phone to the open air so Janine could hear.

"She should take lessons," Janine said.

"Nobody in our family takes lessons," Stan said. "We're all self-taught. That's why we're all—" All what? "We're all a bit tilted."

It wasn't such a bad word. Wasn't the planet tilted? Silence from her.

Was *she* tilted? The way Jason Biggs meant?

Another thought intruded. He really liked talking with her. He was terrible on the phone but he really liked talking with *her*.

He didn't want to hear her say anything to ruin that.

"What about tonight?" he said.

"Uh . . . this dance." Her voice was tight. "It's . . . well, the whole group is, uh . . ."

Clink, clank, slam, clatter . . .

"Lily!" Stan's mother called out from the bathroom. She had her hair roped back and she was wearing the tired purple sweatsuit she always wore for housecleaning.

" . . . they're a bit weird," Janine said. "It's just . . . I wanted to warn you. There might be some . . . parents there."

More silence. "You said your parents were organizing," he said finally. "So I kind of figured they'd be there."

"And that's okay?" She sounded relieved.

"Sure," he said. "I think I already knew."

"I just wasn't sure if I told you," she said quickly.

"Lily, stop it!" Stan's mother screamed. "Stanley!"

"I'm on the phone!" Stan yelled. He pulled the cord around the corner into the dining room.

"You don't have to come if you don't want to," Janine said.

For a gulping moment Stan thought he could smell her. She seemed to be standing too close to him again, and the scent of her pushed his body against the doorframe.

"Why wouldn't I want to come?"

Another long pause. Finally, "I'm not sure about the band," Janine said in a small voice.

She didn't want him to come. She was calling to get him to uninvite himself.

Stan felt a surge of ornery spine.

"Well, like you said, we could go for a walk if we don't like the music."

"I think it's supposed to rain." She had the voice of a girl he desperately wanted to hold in the dark all alone and press his lips up against hers and taste—

What would she taste like?

Stupid. She was calling to call it off. Head in the game, Dart!

"Are you still there?" she asked.

"If you don't think I should come why don't you just say it?" Stan said with too much voice. It hurt not to slam the phone down.

"That's not what I mean," she said.

What, what, what? Stan held the phone away from his ear and hollered at Lily to be quiet.

"I mean," Janine said, "it's a bit of a weird group, but if you're okay with it I'd like you to come."

"How weird?" Stan asked.

"No more weird than my family and me," she said, and he had the sense that he wasn't going to get any more from her than that.

"I wouldn't miss it for the world," he said.

13

IT WAS RAINING BY NOON when Ron showed up again, this time not alone. A little boy was holding onto his hand. They looked like drowned rats on the front porch—a huge soaked, sorry gray Papa Rat with a battered brown suitcase almost as wet as his shirt, and the Boy Rat with jug ears and liquidy black eyes so solemn as he gazed up and up even as rain from his plastered black hair dripped down his face.

Stan stood blocking the door, not knowing what to do.

"Dad," he said.

"Stanley, I'd like you to meet your half-brother. Feldon, this is Stanley."

Feldon reached up a small hand. Stan took it: limp and cold. He remembered his father insisting he, too, learn how to shake hands.

"What are you doing here?" Stan asked.

Ron stood still for a time, dripping.

"Didn't you tell Mom that Feldon was with Kelly-Ann?"

Silence. Ron looked dignified, somehow, gripping that suitcase.

"She's not going to let you stay here. No way," Stan said.

In any contest it was essential to know before-hand what the outcome would be. Where had Stan read that? On some martial arts site. It was a mat-ter of imposing your will on the other, of being cer-tain within yourself that no matter how difficult the struggle, you would prevail.

Stan's father seemed to be imposing his will on him right now.

A gust of wind brought a spray of cold under the shelter of the porch. Stan couldn't keep them stand-ing there forever.

"There's no room for you," Stan heard himself say without conviction. "I mean, Mom has a boy-friend now . . ."

Feldon coughed then. He put his tiny fist up to his mouth and his skinny body curled into a spasm of suf-fering. Ron did not lower his gaze from Stan, but only put a soothing hand on the younger son's shoulder.

"Who is it, Stanley?" his mother called.

She was in her horrendous sweatsuit with her hair roped back and her knitted yellow sockettes. She was going to—

"*Don't let them in!*" she shrieked from the hallway. "*Jesus, Stanley! Don't you*—"

Feldon kept coughing. The wind blew colder than ever.

"Kelly-Ann has abandoned us," Ron said quietly. He knelt down and hugged Feldon until the coughing subsided. Had he ever held Stan like that?

Stan felt his shoulder being tugged back, and then his mother replaced him on the threshold.

"What the fuck are you doing here? Ron, what the *fuck*—?"

Feldon turned his black marvels on her.

"Isabelle, this is Feldon," Ron said. His voice seemed to hold a quiet, triumphant sort of defeat. "Kelly-Ann is gone. Shut us out. We just need a roof for a bit."

"What? You took the bus home and just found this out, and now you're back already? Or you came yesterday and didn't tell me you'd brought your other son?"

Ron stayed on one knee, pleading with his eyes.

"*Why can't you just fucking answer me?*"

Suddenly the wind sent a hanging basket spinning off its hook. It crashed close to Ron and Feldon and splashed black, wet earth on their soaked trousers and shoes. But neither of them flinched.

Coughing, coughing. Once more wretched Feldon clutched his father's rain-soaked shirt.

It was Lily who burst from nowhere, squirmed past her mother and tugged at Feldon's skinny arm.

"Are you Feldon? What are you staying out here for? You need a hot bath and a blankie!"

———

IT WAS AS IF THEY'D taken two strands of a live wire and pressed them together, hoping for an explosion. Ron — Stan's father! — was in the bathroom running hot water for Feldon, the kid who'd split apart the whole family. It was the same bathroom Stan's mother had just cleaned. And Lily was hanging onto the half-open door, looking in, not looking in, and singing in her loud, off-key little-girl voice, "F-L-D-O-N . . . and Feldon was his name — oh!"

"E! E!" Stan wanted to shout.

His mother hovered in the middle of the living room, that hand bunching her roped-up hair, bunching it and releasing. The other hand was holding a glass of wine—at hardly past noon on a Saturday!

Rain hit the windows like liquid shotgun blasts.

"How can this be happening?" she asked.

Maybe Feldon was truly sick. Maybe he'd have to stay in the hospital. Maybe Ron could stay with him, too . . .

"I'm going to have to call Kelly-fucking-Ann," Stan's mother said. "Can you believe it? My husband leaves me. He knocks up a younger woman. And now she's thrown him out . . . and I'm the one who has to hold it together!"

" . . . and Feldon was his name, oh!" sang Lily.

What about me, Stan thought. What about Gary? You haven't done this all alone.

" . . . What do I get for all my trouble? The asshole is back in *my* house with *his* kid and *his* problems . . . he's incapable . . . he's *incapable* of . . ."

As soon as I'm old enough I'm moving out, Stan thought. When might that be? Maybe sixteen was already old enough? Once he got his license. He could get a job somewhere after school. At the grocery store. He could run items through the scanner and give people their change and help them bag. He could go on welfare. He and Janine could move in together . . .

"F-L-D-O-N . . . and Feldon was his—"

" . . . and now I'm the one who's going to have to call her," his mother concluded.

"Why?" Stan asked.

"Because that's the way the universe is. It doesn't just punish you once. It rubs your face in the dirt and when you try to get up—"

She gestured with her hand, and red wine spilled onto the creamy rug she'd bought from the consignment store for Christmas as a treat for herself.

Stan's eyes bounced once between the stain and his mother, but she didn't notice. That's how bad it was.

"*I* have to call her because Kelly-Ann Wilmer is my punishment for something I did, God knows what. Maybe in another life."

If he left to live with Janine—if he took the job at the grocery store, if there was a job, and became his own man—then he'd be abandoning Lily to a crazy woman.

A crazy woman who had raised him with some semblance of normality despite living a train wreck.

A crazy woman who loved them both more than made any sense whatsoever.

"You don't have to call Kelly-Ann," Stan said.

"Well, who else is going to do it?" His mother glanced down irritably.

Then the whole weight of the world seemed to pull her gaze toward the stain. Her eyes fluttered as if she were about to lose consciousness.

"Did I . . . oh," she sighed, and Stan could almost see the anger seeping from her like water through a child's fingers.

"It's all right, I'll clean it," he said.

But instead of going to the kitchen to stare in the cupboard at the possible rug-cleaning products, he stood in the middle of the room and held her while she wept a warm flood against his shoulder. Her hair brushed against his cheek and made his nostrils itchy.

"I'll call Kelly-Ann," he heard himself say.

Anything to help her stop crying. Her shoulders heaved. She had breasts. Skinny as she was, his mother was pressing her breasts against him.

"You're so big and strong now," she said into his soaked shirt. "I'm so proud of you. If I didn't have you—"

The doorbell then. Who? This was not a good day for answering the door. But at least the interruption allowed Stan to unclinch.

Through the foggy pane he saw a man.

Gary! Stan practically hugged the guy.

"Is everything all right?" Gary said. "I've been phoning and phoning your mom . . ."

When he saw her he crossed the room like a man on a mission, wrapped Stan's mother in his fattish arms and stood there and took it. The sobbing anew, the gibberish that had to come out in gasps and gulps before she could say anything intelligible.

"And . . . and . . . he's right here now. He's brought the boy—Feldon—with him. Can you imagine?"

Maybe *Gary* could talk to Kelly-Ann? Gary could stand at the foul line with his back to the basket and sink the most improbable shot. Maybe Gary was Clark Kent.

But when the two men met—in the middle of the living room, with Stan's mom on her knees scrubbing out the red-wine stain on her favorite rug—it was more like Ice Man vs. Whipped Dog. Ron was wet still from the rain and moved like he'd been kicked in the backside and deserved it. And Gary was trying to hold himself tall, was actually sucking in his stomach.

"I heard your boy's sick," Gary said finally.

"It's just a cough," Ron answered. But Feldon's rattle from the bathroom—where did that kid learn his timing?—disquieted the whole house.

"I'm going to need a towel," Ron said. "We won't be staying long. I just have to catch my breath a bit."

Stan imagined the two men falling to blows. His

father was stronger, but somehow Gary looked like he'd come out on top. Whatever on top would mean in a fight between two aging guys with more belly than wallop.

Why wasn't Ron going to the linen closet to get a towel?

Because it wasn't his house anymore.

"I'll get you a towel," Stan said, and he was unreasonably happy for the few seconds it took him away from unfolding Catastrophe II.

Lily was guarding Feldon in the tub.

"He's got a little nib," she said. "Right between his legs!"

Stan could get a job planting trees in the north woods. A helicopter could set him down in the middle of the tundra and he could walk and walk for miles, stooping and planting. He would follow his own compass. At lunch he'd sit on a rock with pine gum on his cheeks and blackflies clouding his face, and the vast and empty tundra would stretch before him, and the sweat would run inside his clothes, and he'd write a card to Janine:

They say this is God's country, and I know what they mean.

And his heart would pound just to think of her, back in civilization, a million miles away.

———

STAN BROUGHT THE TOWEL and Lily loudly rubbed trembling Feldon's goose-pimply body with it. It was hard to tell just what exactly the adults were saying to each other in the living room.

Stan didn't really want to know.

"Do you want to have a lie-down, buddy?" Stan said to Feldon. "Do you want to curl up in bed?"

"Feldon can't talk!" Lily whispered.

"Sure he can," Stan said. Then, to Feldon, "You're just a bit shy getting to know us."

He had the eyes of a hundred-year-old. Not a hint of a smile from his gray, calm face.

"Do you have a change of clothes, Feldon?" Downstairs was ominously quiet.

"He has no clothes, and he can't talk," Lily said. "And he's got the brain of a squirrel!"

Stan tapped Lily's head. "Don't talk about anybody that way," he whispered. "Especially not your half-brother."

Feldon didn't seem to mind.

"Maybe he's half squirrel," Lily said.

Stan found an undershirt for Feldon, whose skin was still cold. Then Stan put him in his own bed, which felt like the brotherly thing to do.

Maybe Stan wouldn't be living there all that much longer anyway, so what would he need his bed for?

"You have a good sleep, Little Man," Stan said. Feldon looked at him like he was never going to close his eyes but it didn't matter. Stan drew the drapes.

He wondered if his father had ever called him Little Man.

———

STAN HAD SAID THAT HE'D call Kelly-Ann, but what was he supposed to say? That her husband Ron had brought Feldon to his ex-wife's house and was on his knees now explaining how to get red-wine stains out of a creamy carpet while his ex-wife's boyfriend paced back and forth looking like he might burst a blood vessel?

Anyway, Stan didn't have the woman's number, and he'd never met her, and for some reason he was having trouble breathing. It felt like a balloon was slowly inflating, crushing him from within.

Ron and Gary looked like they were about to start launching lamps at one another. Probably Stan should stay on hand to protect his mother and the children.

But the inner balloon kept inflating like some maniacal toy.

"It's not coming out!" his mother said.

"Trust me. Trust me, it is!" Ron replied.

What was he rubbing into the carpet? Why was he hunched so badly over the spot so no one else could see?

Why couldn't Stan breathe?

He needed to tell them all that Feldon was in bed upstairs shivering even after the hot bath. And did the boy have a change of clothes?

And he needed to tell his mother, separately, that he wasn't going to call Kelly-Ann. And he needed to tell her that no matter what disaster might be unfolding here, he was going to a dance tonight with Janine Igwash.

And he needed to tell Ron, separately, to get the hell out of their lives. He wanted to have a broom handle in his hand when he did that.

Except he could hardly move right now.

And that's why when Ron, his miserable dad, said, "Son, could you get a little vinegar — not the apple, but the white?" Stan turned and left. The white vinegar was in the closet off the kitchen landing right beside the brooms. If he'd gotten the white vinegar he would have unscrewed the broom handle, too, and murdered his father.

Instead he plunged out the back door into the

driving rain and the whole sweet wide world of fresh air.

Free lungs! He ran and ran. His body was so hot he didn't feel the wet until he was nearly a mile away from the house.

The cold came even later.

14

"I'm Stanley. Stan Dart." Stan tried to keep the trembling from his voice. "You must be Mr. Igwash."

The man at the door stood in a pair of slippers, worn on the outside edges. He didn't have a balanced step. But he towered over Stan. And it looked like his shoulders rubbed both sides of the doorframe at once. His hair was shaved nearly down to his skull. Stan's hand got lost in the big man's grip.

"Do we know you?"

Stan explained that he was Janine's date for the dance. Rainwater washed down his neck even though the worst of the storm was over. The late afternoon had settled into a steady drizzle.

What time was it? What time was he supposed to show up?

Janine's father turned his head slightly. He didn't let his eyes leave Stan's.

"Janine!" he called. He had the holler of a basketball coach. He looked like he could dunk without getting too far off his toes.

Janine appeared in the slight space behind her father's bulk. Her hair was wet and it looked darker. Had she colored it again? Had she been out in the rain herself?

"There's a half-drowned gent here says he's going to the dance with you tonight." Her father's slate gray eyes glimmered with amusement.

"*Daddy*, this is Stan." What was that in her voice? Some little-girl tone Stan hadn't heard from her before.

"Why is Stan all wet? And why is he two and a half hours early?" Janine's dad turned back to Stan. "Are you staying for dinner?"

Stan shifted his weight from one squishy shoe to the other.

"Do you have a change of clothes, son?"

Stan hadn't thought it through. He felt himself shivering like Feldon had on his doorstep just a few hours before.

He didn't want to go back home. Home felt impossibly complicated at the moment.

"Dinner would be delirious," Stan said. Then he laughed. Was this what it was like to be drunk?

They let him in out of the rain. Their house was one half of a duplex—boring brown brick on the outside, spacious and neat on the inside. A hallway immediately offered three choices: left to the living room, straight ahead to the kitchen, where something was cooking, or upstairs to the bedrooms.

Upstairs looked dark.

That's where her dying mother was, Stan thought.

He kicked off his muddy running shoes and stood shivering in the foyer in socks squishy with rainwater. He pulled off those socks, hesitated, then leaned out the door and squeezed them until gray water drenched his wrists and ran onto the porch.

"I can get you something dry," Janine said. "Don't worry. I have lots of boys' clothes."

"Boys' clothes?"

"That's all she would wear for the longest time," her dad said. "Till she started growing in certain directions." His right eye lowered a little when he might be teasing. He had a bony hooked nose that somehow had the same outline as hers, but hers was a lot prettier.

Janine headed up the stairs into the shadows, and her dad stood grinning like he was going to remember this moment for a long, long time.

"Are you coming?" Janine said.

———

THE BATHROOM WAS large and orderly and didn't smell of spilled perfume. Stan looked at himself in the mirror.

Drowned rat. Grinning fool.

She had given him a plaid shirt that fit perfectly and smelled a little like someone adorable had worn it not so long ago. It looked fine on him. It looked better than most of his own shirts.

The jeans were a little long but he could roll up the cuffs, and large at the waist. Janine wasn't a big girl, not in the middle. But he was a skinny guy.

Stan went up for a pretend jump shot in the bathroom. The tips of his fingers brushed the ceiling on his follow-through. Monday morning, six-thirty—rendezvous with destiny. For just a moment he saw himself dribbling the ball through Karl Brolin's legs, then pulling up, fading slightly on the shot. Nothing but net.

Sweetness.

Why did Janine Igwash wear boys' clothes?

Because she could wear anything and still steal the eyes of most men with a pulse.

Or maybe . . . she was tilted.

Stan stepped slightly back and launched a high side kick at his own reflection in the full-length mirror on the wall by the brown towels. It was a perfectly executed blow that left a footprint at face level but shattered nothing. Mark of a master. He wiped the footprint off with toilet paper, and when that still left a murky smudge he wet the toilet paper and wiped again, and when that left greasy streaks he used his hand, then the tail of Janine's shirt.

The dull, blotchy spot that remained on the mirror was about the size of his own face.

———

DOWN THE DARKENED HALLWAY. Janine's room was at the end with the door closed. Two other bedroom doors loomed. One was to a study, which had a desk and a computer and a nice view of the front lawn. The other room, darkened, had its door only slightly ajar. Stan had the feeling that someone was in there dying.

Stan slid past it, didn't want to look.

He knocked quietly on Janine's door.

"Everything fits," he whispered.

"Great." Her voice sounded cool. Did she want

him to push open the door and come in? "I'll be down in a minute."

Instructions clear.

Stan descended the thickly carpeted steps. In the kitchen Janine's dad whirled amidst controlled confusion. Saucepans bubbled, pots steamed, hot oils spat and hissed while the big man poked, adjusted, fiddled with lids.

"How are you in the kitchen, Stan?" her father asked.

"Do you need any help?" Stan took his hands out of his pockets — out of Janine's pockets — in preparation.

"This is perfectly under control. All I'm saying is a man ought to have at least one dish under his command. One never-fail. Are you a basketball player?"

Stan smiled. "I am, actually."

"Then you know. When the heat's on, you're down to the last shot, the defense is tightening like a vise." Barehanded, Janine's dad picked up a scalding hot iron-handled frying pan. "You need something you can rely on." He waved it like it was a badminton racket. "In the kitchen, for me, it's chicken-leg spaghetti. I wooed Janine's mom on it exclusively. It's dead simple. Buy some spaghetti sauce, pour it in a pan like this, dump in the chicken legs and cook it all slowly. The secret's in the spices. This is true for all of life, practically. Onion, of course. But garlic first. The older you get, the more you put in. Basil. I'm starting to really appreciate basil. And rosemary. Rosemary and chicken are practically a perfect marriage. Peppers—green and red, maybe a little bit of—"

The front door opened and Stan felt the draft pull him around. A woman appeared in a brilliant purple and silver headscarf and a raincoat so yellow it nearly vibrated. She had shopping bags in her hands.

"Not spaghetti chicken again!" she said. She peeled off her coat. "I told you I was handling dinner!" She squinted at Stan. "Janine, honey, what are you wearing? The dance is tonight!"

Janine's dad walked past Stan into the hallway and wrapped the woman in his big arms.

"I've got dinner covered," he said. "And this is Stan—"

She squinted again. "*You're* Stan?"

Stan failed to reply, as if indeed he might be an imposter. The moment grew so awkward that Janine's mother seemed almost forced to say, "I'm sorry. I took my contacts out in the store, they were hurting so much. I'm blind as a bat like this."

She pushed her husband aside and hugged Stan fiercely. She was a tiny woman, mostly bone.

"Janine has a shirt exactly like yours," she said. "Thank God she isn't—"

Suddenly Janine was at the base of the stairs in a killer black dress with a slit up to her waist, practically, and black leggings and a big silver buckle and white cowboy boots.

She was so beautiful, Stan felt his jaw soften, his hinges melt.

Her hair really was black now, and her eyes seemed dark, dark. She didn't look like the same girl at all.

What was she doing going out with Stan?

"I see you've met my mom," Janine said.

Janine's mother was still clenching him.

"I didn't know he was coming for dinner," she said. "But he's got a good feel to him."

———

"THE MAIN THING I tell my clients is, prepare for life. You don't know all the twists and turns. You can't predict every bounce of the ball. But you can prepare your reserve force. That's the key. The single most important investment in almost anyone's life . . ."

Janine's father paused. The four of them were

sitting at a round table in a back alcove—candlelight, linen napkins that seemed to have been starched. Darkness pressing from the outside.

". . . is the home, of course. Cover your mortgage. But that's only the start. What if you lose your job? Or you fall ill? What if—"

"Stan isn't married, dear," Janine's mother—Gillian—said. "He doesn't have children and he doesn't want to think about it for years and years."

"The smart investor," Janine's father went on, "looks at those risks. What about retirement? Okay, you tell me you're sixteen years old. You think retirement is a hundred years away. Do you think the government is going to look after you when you're sixty-five? Consider the deficit. Consider the ominous shifts in global trade—"

"Joe." Gillian placed her thin hand on his long forearm. "Maybe we can talk about other things."

Janine was studying her plate across the table from Stan. Her tiny lizard shoulder tattoo peeked out at him. If this wasn't dinner, if they were alone, he could reach over—if he brushed aside some of her black, black hair . . .

"Tell us about your family, Stan," Gillian said. "What does your father do?"

A slurp of sauce caught in the back of Stan's

throat and he sneezed some of it, without thinking, onto the white linen napkin.

"He's a carpenter," Stan spat out.

"A carpenter!" Gillian exclaimed. "You know, I'd really like to expand the family room. But it's so hard to find someone . . ."

Joe glared at his wife. Janine shook her head slowly, staring a rut into her plate.

"Contractors rip you off," Joe said. "No offense to your father, Stan. But if it's at all possible to do the work yourself . . ."

Gillian snorted. "Two words, dear. *The bathroom*. And three more. *Lest we forget*."

Joe picked up his chicken leg dripping with sauce and tore a chunk from it with his teeth like Henry VIII in some movie.

"The bathroom was years ago. I've learned a lot since the bathroom."

"You have learned to hire a contractor. Somebody who will do it right the first time." Gillian turned to Stan. "How long has your father been a carpenter?"

Stan had to concentrate to pick up his own chicken leg cleanly.

"I'm not really sure. I think only a couple of months. He was in real estate before that, and a lawyer before that."

Silence. Finally Joe said, "A lot of lawyers decide they want to do an honest day's work in midlife."

"You just said most contractors are shysters," Gillian said to her husband.

"For God's sake!" Joe said. "I'm getting to know Janine's boyfriend."

Stan felt all eyes on him again now. Was he supposed to say something? Silence stretched like ice taking over the room. Then the words just popped out of him.

"My father left us five years ago and never sent a dollar to help my mom with my sister and me. I never talk to him, he never writes, he's missed every birthday since I was eleven. Then yesterday he just showed up again, and today he brought Feldon, my half-brother."

Stan sucked the chicken bone. He was breathing like a marathon runner.

"They're all back there right now in the living room. My mom, her boyfriend, Gary, Ron—that's my dad. I wouldn't be surprised if World War III has broken out. That's why I showed up early." He wiped his fingers properly on the napkin. "This is really delicious," he said.

Gillian was trembling.

"You poor boy," she said. "You're getting the full wallop."

"The what?"

"Life's all hitting at once. The way it does sometimes. That's why we all need to go out dancing."

Stan glanced at Janine, then back at her mom.

"The universe kicks you in the teeth and the only thing to do is dance like crazy. You'll see. Tonight is going to be a huge release!"

15

THEY DROVE IN THE rainy dark. Stan sat in the back behind Gillian. As soon as Janine clicked her seatbelt shut she reached across to Stan and their fingers interlaced again. Stan started to come to a boil from the inside.

Then Gillian coughed so hard her little body shook the car. When it was over she stretched back awkwardly for a moment to view Stan. She smiled when she saw their hands.

The car kept going. Janine squeezed tighter.

Maybe he really was Janine's boyfriend?

"Your mother must be an amazing woman to raise the both of you on her own," Gillian said.

Was his mother amazing? Maybe. But what Stan ended up explaining was that she could never figure out how to work the TV remote no matter how often he explained it.

"My mom has two degrees but when it comes to electronics—"

Gillian asked about the degrees, so Stan said what he could about sociology and the history of art.

"She's a Vermeer freak," he said, and he tried to remember the name of the painting—a copy, obviously—that hung in their living room near the fireplace that didn't work.

"*The Girl with the Pearl Earring*?" Gillian said.

"Not that one. But it looks like that one. My mom could tell you all about it."

Why couldn't Stan tell them all about it? Maybe he didn't pay enough attention to his mother. She was terrifically smart in her own way.

He could feel the pulse in Janine's fingers.

"She used to drag us to galleries all the time. But my little sister is allergic to them. It's like her skin starts to itch from the inside. She just can't stay still. So my mom goes on her own, or else she drags Gary." The wipers sloshed water back and forth without seeming to clear anything. Could Joe see out the windshield at all?

"Gary's great," Janine breathed then. "He let me win at silly basketball." She had the sexiest voice when she was talking quietly.

Let this ride go on and on, Stan thought.

"Did you . . . go to university?" he asked Gillian.

She turned and smiled oddly. "I studied to be an anthropologist, but ended up working in the bank, and then I got sick."

Joe reached across and covered her frail hand gently with his own.

It was a sticky part of the conversation. Stan wasn't sure what he should say next. He felt like he could spill anything about his own family now, that a rusty door had been knocked open. His mother's purple sweatsuit. Gary and Ron like bulls in the living room. Feldon dripping on the porch in the rain.

The wipers sloshed. Janine withdrew her hand. Was he gripping too hard?

"I met Joe at the bank," Gillian said. "I was supervising him, actually. He married me to get ahead."

"I married her to get ahead," Joe chimed. It seemed to be a family joke.

"There was a rule at the time against office dating, so we had to sneak around," Gillian said. "That's the thing about those kinds of rules."

"They encourage the opposite behavior," Joe said.

"We were illicit lovers." Gillian beamed at him now. These two middle-aged people—Joe with his bristly head, Gillian with her scarf and the hard lines on her neck, like the flesh was retreating from her bit by bit—looked like they had more love between them in just this car ride than Stan had ever seen between his own parents.

This was what Janine had grown up with.

He wanted to take her hand again, but suddenly felt shy.

———

THE REC CENTER was a squat brownish building in a part of town Stan didn't recognize. Were they downtown? He couldn't even guess.

As soon as they walked in, Gillian took charge.

"Put the pop table over there!" she said to two boys fiddling with fold-up legs. "Did you bring the banner?"

It was rolled up in a corner, and Gillian had Stan and Janine hang it on the far wall under the shaded windows.

Dance for Life, it said.

Families arrived in noisy clumps. The kids seemed to be of all ages, the girls wearing everything from pants to slinky dresses, the boys in probably whatever they'd had on earlier in the day. So Stan wasn't out of place in Janine's plaid shirt and jeans.

Some of the kids were . . . bald, or otherwise sickly looking.

Or they had a parent who was too thin or trembly and pale, lost in the eyes.

"It's for cancer families," Janine explained. "And guests. My mom just wants everybody to dance their brains out."

She gave him a nervous glance. A flash of a smile that was a firefly zipping past a window.

Gillian gave him exactly the same smile a moment later when she was wrestling a cooler into place all by herself. Stan hurried over to help her.

"I really like the look of you," she said. "Janine has never had a boyfriend before."

That word again. *Boyfriend.*

"For a while we wondered if she would ever get one," Gillian said.

———

STAN WASN'T A DANCER. He'd been to a couple of school events, had stood in the shadows shifting his weight from side to side, wishing he were somewhere else. But here everybody danced: parents, kids, old folks, teenagers. The whole crowd wriggled and shook with their hands in the air.

They all seemed to be laughing and smiling in the sweaty semidarkness.

So Stan bounced on his heels and let his shoulders jiggle around and his pec muscles—if that's what they were—quiver and his hands flap. It was all by feel. A musician in black jeans bopped between an electric guitar, some drums and the microphone. A skinny girl with orange hair sang and blew sometimes on a harmonica. Most of the words were unrecognizable— "Going to ax my kaleidoscope" was one line that stayed in Stan's head.

"Who are they?" he screamed across at Janine, but she couldn't hear. She danced with her eyes closed a lot of the time, and her body was . . . fluid. Everything melted together, like waves moving in wax that hardened slightly then melted again into something else.

Before too long the band took a break but the music continued—some kid's computer hooked up to the sound system. Stan was taken by surprise when a slow song came on. Couples just seemed to fall together, but Stan felt like he couldn't fall. He was a wooden post stuck in the ground. Janine wasn't standing next to him, anyway. She was a few paces off. Waiting?

Wasn't this what he'd come for? Wouldn't a

real boyfriend just walk over and they would cling together and shuffle their feet the way other people did?

Except Joe and Gillian weren't shuffling their feet. They were waltzing. Was that what it was? Gliding. She barely came to chest height on her husband, but how straight they both stood, how buttery their movements looked.

They were really *dancing*.

Stan couldn't compete with that. He stood a bit behind Janine and watched those two dip and glide. Then he clapped with all the others when the song was over.

"Your parents are amazing!" he said. But Janine rolled her eyes. Maybe nobody thought their own parents were amazing.

When the band came back, Stan just started bouncing. Janine shimmied and melted and spun more or less on her own. He tried to bounce in time with the way she was moving her shoulders. But then she would break it off and dance with somebody else—with a tiny girl in a white dress and black shoes who had her own way of moving. She would dip her shoulder and sway back, then throw her hands in the air. Stan threw his hands, too, but thought he probably looked like he was going for a rebound so he stopped. Better to just let his hands dangle at the end of his arms.

Janine had said she wasn't much of a dancer. What an outright lie that was! A fish in a pool couldn't have looked more graceful.

He was the one who didn't know what he was doing.

He bounced closer to her.

"Janine!" he yelled, two inches from her ear.

She vibrated with the girl in the white dress and didn't hear him.

"Janine!" He brushed against her shoulder. She opened her eyes like she was waking up from something pleasant.

" . . . mini-mega mall mart monkeys," the singer seemed to be screaming.

"What?"

"You're a great dancer!" he yelled.

" . . . making like rogue-wing flunkies," the singer screeched.

"What?"

"You're a . . ."

Suddenly the wall of sound collapsed into rubble and everyone was clapping. Janine hugged the white-dress girl—who gave Stan a bit of a sour look—and Stan's voice broke.

160 | Alan Cumyn

"... a great dancer," he said pitifully.

No reply. Janine and the girl unclenched. Something slow started up. The band was much better loud and rough. They should have left the soft stuff to the recorded music. Stan steeled himself to—to what? He was already close enough to put his arms around Janine. He was so close his arms would have gone around the white-dress girl, too. She and Janine had an eye thing going—a secret message telegraphed between them.

Stan felt something in his belly turn sour.

A boyfriend at this point would just say, "Wanna dance?" And Janine would throw her arms around him . . .

"Do you want to get a drink?" Janine said to him instead.

What *did* he want?

He wanted to breathe in her intoxication. He wanted her to bury her head in the hollow of his shoulder. She was a little taller than him but it still might work.

He wanted the music to be so much better than this. He wanted to open his eyes slowly and find that her mouth was searching for his. What would that be like?

He wanted . . .

He wanted to not be standing all alone in the middle of everything—of nothing—while she moved off to get a cup of juice.

———

AND THEN SHE DISAPPEARED. One moment she was sipping from a paper cup and the white-dress girl bumped her elbow and Janine splashed something on her own killer dress. It was black, anyway. How much could show in a darkened auditorium? And then the two of them were heading off to the washroom. So Stan went to the men's room and checked himself out in the mirror. He looked stupid, and the jeans didn't fit. With that belt cinched tight and the cuffs rolled up he looked like a farmer.

He needed to call his mom to tell her where he was. If he had a cellphone he'd call her right from there, in the men's can.

It smelled of wine and someone's cigarette.

Those same muscles that had run out the back door at home now wanted to run out of this suffocating place.

She'd held his hand most of the way on the rainy car ride here.

Why hadn't he just said, "Wanna dance?"

He didn't know any steps. But she would have rested her head in the hollow of his shoulder and they would have clutched and shuffled, welded together for infinity.

———

BACK IN THE DARK AGAIN, the music still tortured the air. Next slow dance, whatever it was, he'd just grab her and everything else would disappear.

Where was she, anyway?

Stan couldn't see her on the dance floor. The whole crowd was up writhing, wriggling, Gillian and Joe in the middle, clutched like lovers.

Stan didn't know where to stand, what to do, where to put his hands. He shuffled over to the drink table. It was fifty cents for an apple juice and he had nothing in his pockets.

They were Janine's pockets.

He smiled dopily at the guy behind the table and backed away as if he'd planned all along to pick up one of the paper cups and look at it and put it down again without drinking or paying.

No harm no foul.

There she was! Janine exited the girls' room with the white-dress girl.

The girl was welded up against her. Janine took the girl's hand and removed it from her waist.

Stan felt like he was in a movie all of a sudden. Janine dropped the girl's arm and looked around the room—searching for him?—but she couldn't see him. She was real, he was in a movie, this was all happening and it wasn't.

She liked girls. Simple as that. He'd known it and had fooled himself into not knowing it. The truth of it was like a ball bouncing hard off the rim straight down into his face.

She'd dragged Stan to this dance to be a cover for . . . for what?

She was scanning the room, looking for him. But he was turned to nothing.

Janine saw him trying to push through. He felt stopped but his body kept going. Past the writhing, dancing families, out the doors into hard rain but night now, too, and again no umbrella, no jacket.

Where?

Feet slipping on the pavement. It was a drenched street in an unknown part of the city. There was Janine's parents' car parked with dozens of others. Why hadn't he paid attention to where they were going? It was colder even than it had been that afternoon. But he was running.

He was going to cramp up soon. He was going too fast. Lactic acid was crackling his muscles.

He didn't know what the hell was going on.

"Hey!" someone called out miles behind him. So far back he could easily not have heard her.

Breathe, stride-stride-stride, *breathe* . . .

"Hey!" she called from farther back.

He didn't have to stop. He could just have slowed and even then she would never catch him.

She was in her killer dress but she looked like a soggy shadow except for her white boots.

She probably wasn't much of a runner. But she'd come after him.

"Where are you going?" she said.

"Why didn't you tell me?" he shot back.

Her shoulders were bare and wet. She had to be bloody freezing.

Her chest was heaving. She had a glorious chest. He wasn't sure she was going to be able to say anything.

He thought maybe she was going to try to lie about what he'd seen.

But instead she said, "I'm sorry."

She was standing in her killer black dress with her black hair plastered to her white, white face a few paces off, like she was about to draw her pistol and shoot him dead. He was already shot through.

16

He had known that going to the dance would be a whole bigger deal than it should have been.

"Sorry about what?"

She was crying in the rain. When he was the one who should be upset. Was this the way all girls operated?

"I broke it off with Leona weeks ago and then she came tonight anyway and I couldn't keep her away." She wiped her face. "My parents don't know *anything*. Please don't tell them. I thought . . . I thought asking you was the right thing."

"For what?"

"My mother has gone through second chemo. She only has about two months to live. That's what all the doctors say. She lives for these dances. She just shines. But she'll be days and days in bed afterwards. And I know she wanted me to invite one boy I liked. Just one."

"But you like girls?"

She was shivering and crying and not answering.

He'd seen the two of them dancing together. He'd seen the white-dress girl—Leona—with her arm around Janine.

"I like boys, too," Janine said. "Maybe. I like you." She shivered deeply.

Clearly, despite everything, it was his duty to hold her, warm her. "I called *you*," she said. "I wanted to go with you."

It was his duty but he couldn't move. It felt like . . . rigor mortis was setting in. If she wanted him to hold her, to warm her . . .

Even as the argument presented itself in his mind, she somehow curled into his arms. How did that happen? She felt . . . quite warm and soft in all the right places. She clutched him and even though they weren't moving it was almost as if the two of them were slow dancing after all. Her words were terribly sad and the sound of them—the feel of her—had a different effect.

"So . . . you do like me?" he said. The words fell out. Stupidly, pathetically.

"Of course."

There was no reason to stay clenched wherever they were—in the middle of the street, practically. He, too, was starting to shake with the night's cold.

How confused was this? But the feel of her now . . . her hands on the small of his back, pulling him firmly against her middle.

"I saw you looking at me in class," she whispered. "Guys think we don't notice or something."

This close there was no focus. This close they could say anything.

It was odd. Any moment a truck was going to split the darkness with its headlights and crush their bones.

YOUNG COUPLE KILLED IN MIDDLE OF THE ROAD!

His mother would evaporate with shock and grief.

But now they were slow-motion dancing.

None of this made any sense.

And neither did the kiss. It only took each of them to move slightly. At first she turned her cheek a bit toward his, and he edged away because he didn't know if she wanted to kiss him. She pressed closer. Then he couldn't turn any farther. Once on a science class nature trip in elementary school he'd seen a brown owl—at a nature center, in a big pen—turn his head farther, farther, until he'd almost cork-screwed it completely around. But at 270 degrees or so—was that possible?—the owl swiveled his head the other way.

So Stan turned back to her and at first their lips just collided, the way two people pass in a crowded corridor when they aren't paying attention. An accident, then . . .

Lock.

Her lips were terribly smooth and cold at first, then wondrously warm. If he kept his eyes open the rain crept in, so he closed them and held her even tighter. She was very strong. She had an enormous grip on . . . on all of him. But she didn't move her head or lips around. She had . . . smooth teeth. He could taste the sweet juice.

She was kissing him.

And it wasn't making a lot of sense.

Her tongue was . . . and his was . . . and every-thing was . . .

A car honked then, God! It swerved hard and could have hit them. Stan pulled Janine over to the sidewalk. Where they should have been all the time.

KISSING TEENS BREATHE THEIR LAST!

They stood apart now. Stan had no idea what his

face looked like, but Janine's was . . . astonished. Her mouth was hanging open.

And then she was running, running back to the dance. She was fast, too. It was surprising how strong her stride was.

She could run track. She could run track in a black dress and cowboy boots.

I should go after her, Stan thought.

Because that kiss meant something.

It wasn't what she'd expected.

His very first kiss. Maybe hers, too. With a boy.

She was a block away already when he started after her. She was fast but he was faster.

Or he should have been. If he wasn't so cold. And wet. His pants—her pants on him—were soaked and grabbed at his legs. He was a better runner than this, but she was pulling away.

She hadn't said anything about being a track star.

She made it to the door of the rec center far ahead of him, and that changed things somehow. She was running away—away from *him*—so he had no right to follow. She was back safe with her family . . . with her girlfriend, Leona.

She kissed him, then chose her.

And Stan *did* know where he was. May Creek Boulevard was just over there. It would be a long

walk but he'd make it home. May Creek to Edding-
ton and then he'd hit the river and it would be only
a couple more miles from there.

He'd been Janine Igwash's boyfriend for about
fifteen minutes. That had to be some kind of record.

17

When Stan staggered down the stairs the next day at three o'clock in the afternoon, wiping the sleep from his eyes, the house was empty except for his father taking apart the toilet.

"What are you doing?" Stan asked.

His father was on his knees surrounded by greasy tools, and the toilet lay on its side like an upended ship. A dark hole ringed by yellowy black wax stared up from the bathroom floor. The sewer reek was far worse than the leftover Chanel disaster upstairs.

"I'm trying to save your mother a substantial amount of money," Ron said. "You know how much water these relics use in a year?"

Stan didn't know. His father's hands were covered in the yellowy black wax, a dab of which dangled from his cheek as well.

"You disappeared last night," Ron said. "Your mother's going to kill you when she gets back." Ron explained that they had all gone to the art gallery: Stan's mother, Lily, Feldon and Gary.

"Isn't Feldon sick?" Stan asked.

"Miraculous recovery. Must be something in the air around here."

Could he not smell anything?

Stan couldn't figure out what Ron was doing with the toilet. He just seemed to be wiping grease on himself, a rag, the tools, the rag again . . .

"So it's . . . pretty serious with this guy, I guess," Ron said. "Gary."

What was his father fishing for?

"They've been together what—a couple of months?" Ron's eyes didn't stay on a person. They darted here and there. And why did he just keep wiping himself?

"Longer than a couple of months," Stan said.

"I bet he doesn't play hockey," Ron pressed. "Guy looks like he'd fall flat on his ass if you put him in a pair of skates."

Stan and his father did play hockey together. Stan remembered the cold on his face in the morning at the outdoor rink, the slap of the puck against the boards, how hot they would get in just a few minutes of hard skating.

"Gary is . . . surprising in a lot of ways," Stan said.

"I wish your mother was," Ron muttered. He shifted from his knees and sat on the side of the tub, his body hunched forward as if they were in the change hut after a full morning of chasing the puck. "Your mother is completely predictable, I hate to say."

Why didn't he cover the hole? The entire house was going to stink.

"She's hard-assed. Pardon my French. Fucking unforgiving."

Stan couldn't help himself.

"You left us," he said. "You started a family with somebody else. Why would you think Mom would forgive you for that?"

Ron shook his head slowly. "It's not a simple world, kid. Sometimes people pretend it is. Kelly-Ann is a piece of work, let me tell you. She turned my head, then she got herself pregnant, and if I didn't go with her . . ."

The thought hovered in the bathroom like the swamp gas.

"What?"

"She was threatening to kill herself. *And* the baby. My hands were tied. I put up with it as long as I could."

"So, you took Feldon? Does Kelly-Ann know you're here?"

"I'm just doing what's good for the boy." Somehow another blob of yellowy black appeared on Ron's chin. "And if your mother has no room in her heart for forgiveness, well . . ."

Ron glanced to either side of Stan's face, his eyes never settling.

"A man does according to his nature," Ron said. "You'll figure that out. Probably exactly what you were doing last night. Tomcatting, my father used to call it. You never knew your grandfather. He was a tough old bastard. But we've all got it in us. What you asked me the other night on the phone. That's the family curse right there. Women don't understand and they don't fucking forgive and the next thing you're out in the cold."

Something was not right in those eyes, in the way his hands kept moving, wiping here, rubbing there. As if he didn't know entirely what he was doing.

Ron tapped the side of the gaping hole with a wrench.

"I thought maybe this wasn't going to be a standard size. And I was right. It's not. I know some things, you see. I fucking do."

A sound then from the front of the house. His mother and the rest getting back from the gallery. Stan went to the front hall as they came in all together.

Feldon did look recovered. He was carrying a small bag with the gallery's logo on it. Probably they'd bought postcards in the gift shop.

Gary seemed to be chewing on words he didn't want to let out.

"Daddy!" Lily said and pushed past Stan to the bathroom. Had she come unsprung at the gallery as usual?

His mother glanced at Stan—cold-eyed—shook out her umbrella and hung up her coat.

Not a word.

That's how bad it was.

Gary nodded to him grimly, then shuffled in the hallway.

"I . . . I'll call you tonight," he said to Stan's mother.

"You better," she said. And they kissed. It wasn't earth-shattering. It wasn't like Stan's kiss. The memory of it zinged through his body like an uncoiling spring.

Then Gary was gone, and Stan's mother banged cupboards in the kitchen. Not good.

Ron wanted back into the family! But he didn't deserve it.

Anyone could see that.

Feldon came up to Stan with his big eyes and his long face. "You snore!"

"How would you know?" Stan asked gently. Feldon seemed to be wearing new clothes.

"Because!" Feldon scrunched his nose and made snuffling noises, which caused Stan to remember vaguely that the dark bed had been lumpy in the middle of the night when he'd slumped in.

Of course! He'd put Feldon in it himself the day before. Feldon with a fever, this same boy now balancing on one leg and scratching his nose.

"How are you feeling?" Stan put his hand on the boy's forehead. Not boiling. Stan remembered being sick like Feldon when he was little and then the next day being perfectly fine.

Feldon blew through his lips and hopped around the room with his arms open like an airplane.

Better, apparently.

"Want to go fishing?" Stan asked.

The thought just occurred to him as he spoke it—a stroke of genius. They still had two rods in the basement. Stan thought he knew where. And the tackle box was in the laundry room under the old table.

"I know a place," Stan said. "If you don't get a bass, at least you'll get a sunfish."

Feldon the airplane continued to circle as if out of radio contact.

How badly was it raining? Nothing like last night.

His mother couldn't possibly stay mad at him if he took the kid out. And if they left, his mother would say what she needed to say to Ron, who would realize this wasn't his house anymore. Even if he did, replace the toilet.

Stan headed down to the basement to gather the gear. The rods were on shelves behind several boxes of Christmas ornaments. It was a matter of moving a few things . . .

"The new one won't fit," Stan heard his father say to his mother on the main floor.

The heating vent was right over his head. They might as well have been using a loudspeaker.

"I don't believe this," his mother said.

"It's a standard size, but the pipes here aren't standard."

"I don't believe this," his mother said again.

"There is an adapter. But I have to go back to the store."

"Did you call her?"

"I think it'll be all right."

"Did you call her?"

There were the fishing rods. Stan had no reason to stay under the vent, but he lingered, anyway.

"She's pretty adamant," Ron said.

"About what? Leaving you? What about Feldon?"

Maybe Stan could just get Feldon out quietly. He wouldn't have to say where they were going.

"Ron! Say something!"

He could just leave a note, maybe.

"What did you do to get her so angry at you? Did she really leave you, or did you leave her and take Feldon with you?"

If Ron was explaining, Stan couldn't hear it. Feet moved over his head.

"It's just a simple adapter," said Ron. Heavy footsteps down the hall. Then the front door opened and shut.

Stan got the tackle box and silently climbed the stairs again. Feldon wasn't buzzing around anymore. He didn't seem to be anywhere. Stan quietly called for him in the kitchen. Ron had gone — probably to the hardware to get the adapter. Did he take Feldon?

"Where are *you* going?" His mother stood blocking the passage to the front door, her hands on her hips. The rims of her eyes were dangerously red.

"I'm sorry," Stan said.

"Yesterday you just walked out! You dragged yourself back in the middle of the night . . ." If she grimaced any further her jaw was going to crack.

"I'm sorry," he said again. He felt pretty foolish

standing in the kitchen with a couple of fishing rods. Especially if Feldon was gone.

"You just disappeared! Do you have any idea—?"

"I'm sorry! I'm sorry!" Bits of dust fell from the spin-caster onto the kitchen floor. Stan watched the clumps fall, then wondered if he should pick them up or if that would make things worse.

"Where did you go?"

Stan's eyes went down to the dust clumps anyway. Just for a second. The counter door was slightly open. And there was Feldon cowering with his eyes closed and his hands over his ears.

The sight of the boy drained all the counterpunch from him.

"I told you I was going to a dance," Stan said. "I should have called. I'm sorry. I didn't think—"

He was going to say he didn't think she'd miss him, but of course that wasn't true.

"You didn't think!" she said. "You didn't think! Now look!" She gestured toward the bathroom as if somehow, if he'd been there, Stan would have prevented the whole disaster. "He's getting me to spend two hundred dollars on a new toilet that doesn't fit and I don't bloody well need!"

Stan wanted to just take Feldon by the hand and pull him out.

"I went to the dance and I got home a little late," he said. "I'm sorry."

Lily came down the stairs clutching Mr. Strawberry.

"Fishing!" she cried.

"I was going to take Feldon down to the river," Stan said.

"What about me!" Lily said, like her mouth was spring-loaded.

Lily, who hated fishing.

Feldon closed the cupboard door a little farther on himself.

Light rain fell on the window.

"I never get to go fishing!" Lily wailed.

———

"Did you ever do this with your dad?" Stan asked as they headed down the sidewalk toward the river. He was holding Feldon's hand. Feldon had the tackle box and Lily had Mr. Strawberry and the smaller rod, which she kept swishing dangerously. If he wasn't careful she would poke somebody's eye out.

"I saw it on TV," the boy said.

"But your dad never took you out? He never left you on the dock or anything?" Stan felt like a prosecutor pulling on an uncertain line of questioning.

"We went to a store once," Feldon said.

"A fishing store?"

"I want to go to the Tilt-the-World!" Lily cried.

Stan looked where she was pointing. Across the street at the Longworth Mall, a lone groaning silver ride glinted and whirled in a fenced-off section of parking lot. A few kids screamed, but most of the swinging arms of the mechanical beast were empty.

"It's probably not safe in the rain," Stan said. "Mom would never let you."

"You couldn't afford to take us anyway!" Lily said. She poked Feldon on the shoulder. "Nobody has any money. Not in our family!"

"My mommy has money," Feldon said.

Stan grabbed Lily's wrist and pulled both kids across an intersection.

"She's going to come get me," Feldon said.

"Does she even know where you are?" Stan asked.

"Why wouldn't she know?" Lily demanded. She was allowing herself to be led.

"We play secrets a lot," Feldon said.

"What kind of secrets?" Stan pressed.

Feldon started to hum a little tune, then flattened his lips together like he would not talk no matter what happened.

The river was only a few blocks away. Stan steered the kids around a deep puddle.

He stopped and kneeled down to look Feldon in the eye.

"This is important. Does your mom know where you are?"

Feldon shook his head and stared down at his shoes. But what he said was, "My mom knows everything."

———

LILY CAST INTO THE TREES, into the weeds, into a bush beside Feldon's head, and Stan took the fishing rod from her so she ran onto a log by the river's edge where faeries hid and talked to them for quite a while on her belly with the ties from her raincoat dragging into the edge of the water.

Feldon opened and closed the tackle box, opened and closed it, and took out each colorful, prickly lure, his little fingers wonderful at avoiding every barb. He lined up the spinners and the leaders and the big hooks and the bobbers, the lead weights, the rubber worms and the spoons. They were like an army in the grass, or a specialized audience come to watch while Stan cast out beyond the shallows and slowly reeled in, cast out and reeled in.

So much was happening, and yet it was not long before he was thinking again of Janine. What did she do after the kiss, when she got back to the dance with Leona?

Did she kiss Leona the way she kissed him?

Why hadn't she told him it was a cancer dance? She was a good talker. Why did he have to get there to find out?

Why didn't she tell him about . . . the girl thing? Everyone knew anyway. Even Jason Biggs.

What else didn't Stan know about her?

"*Lily!*" Stan called out. She was leaning out to the water, her foot planted in mud.

"I have to get the ship back!" she said.

Stan grabbed her arm just as she was slipping. The "ship" was a pine cone spinning in the current out of reach.

Stan picked up another one and handed it to her.

"That's not the ark of Ignola!" she said. She threw it in the water.

"The ark of Igwash," Stan muttered.

"What are you talking about?" Lily said. "You don't know anything!"

He did know some things. He knew, whatever it was with Janine, that kiss was real. A person could run away from it, but that didn't mean it wasn't important.

A kiss like that changed lives. You didn't just give up on it.

"I hate fishing!" Lily said, splashing her hand in the water. "Why did we ever come?"

"It helps you think," Stan said.

18

IT WAS CANNED bean soup for dinner but Stan didn't care. He was so hungry he shoveled the brown mush into his mouth and washed it down with water. Prison rations, practically. But the biscuits were fresh-bought not frozen, and his mother had warmed them.

They were all sitting together in what just two days ago would have seemed an impossible scene: his mother and father at the same table, drinking wine—Gary's from the other night—with three children now instead of two, everyone eating in thick silence. Stan felt like he was in one of those parallel science-fiction universes where characters suddenly found that elements in their lives had become subtly altered, perhaps for evil reasons.

His father had a beard and was eating bean soup.

They always had meat and potatoes when he lived with them.

Feldon, his new brother, was leaning both skinny elbows on the table.

His real father would have straightened him up.

His mother had not thrown Ron and Feldon out of the house yet. Instead she had put on a nice blouse and Gary wasn't even around. Gary had been replaced by Ron.

No one was saying anything about it.

Or about the new toilet, which was in place but not to be flushed, apparently.

"So how were the fish biting, Stanley?" his father asked.

Lily sneezed prodigiously all over everybody's food.

"I don't think they caught anything but colds," Stan's mother said.

Stan wiped his bowl clean with a last bit of biscuit. Was there more? He felt like Oliver Twist.

One wrong word and the whole fishbowl was going to explode.

"Can I bring Feldon to school tomorrow and show him to my friends?" Lily asked in her sweetest voice. Mucus hung from her nostril.

"Wipe your nose, please," his mother said. "Feldon

is not anybody's show and tell. Your father and Feldon will be moving on. Maybe tomorrow?" She eyed Ron, but he kept eating.

He was not sitting at the head of the table. He seemed a lot smaller than he used to.

"Your father called Kelly-Ann this afternoon," Stan's mother announced in an all-is-under-control voice. She passed around a salad that no one wanted. The leafy greens were a bit black on the edges. Ron moved it aside. "Everything's straight. Isn't it, Ron?" she said.

Ron seemed fascinated with his last crust of biscuit.

"You figure you'll be heading home in the next couple of days." Stan's mother hardened her eyes toward Ron.

"Or sooner," Ron said brightly. He was not a bright man—Stan could see that now. When a dim man suddenly became bright, something was wrong.

A car passed in the street with headlights blazing, and the parallel universe held. Lily finally wiped her nose with a napkin and Feldon blew little bubbles onto his spoon.

The phone rang then and Stan wished it was Janine. Maybe she was calling to say she'd been thinking about him all day, really thinking, and had decided she wasn't a lesbian after all.

Nobody moved at the table. The phone rang, rang.

"Why do people phone during the dinner hour?" Stan's mother said.

Stan heard his own voice from the answering machine in the kitchen inviting the caller to say a few words after the beep.

Beep.

No words.

"Telemarketers," Stan's mother said.

Maybe. But why were they the last family in civilization not to have call display?

Money. That was why.

Lesbians didn't just decide to not be lesbians anymore. Did they? Stan felt foggy on the subject. Some people were bi. Did they know at this age?

Maybe Janine was just trying him out. Her first boy.

Maybe she ran away after the kiss because she was confused.

Maybe she was waiting by the phone, wondering if he would call.

He'd never called her. Maybe that's what she wanted now.

Feldon studied his spoon. He had hardly eaten anything.

Then Ron looked at everyone with his droopy eyes and said, "I just wanted to tell you how much it means to me to be here. We're all family. I know it's hard to deal with sometimes, but in the end it's all we've got. I really believe that."

Feldon dropped his spoon, and brown mush soup oozed onto the floor. Nobody moved. Stan's mother was looking at her husband—at her ex-husband —with such . . . what?

Like he'd just boiled the children in the bath water.

"*You are so full of*—" She threw down her utensils and bolted. *Clump, clump, clump* went her heavy feet on the stairs. The walls shuddered with the slamming of the bedroom door.

Ron finished his biscuit carefully. Stan had the sense he wasn't exactly sure where his next meal might be coming from.

———

THE TELEPHONE IN THE kitchen beckoned, but there were too many bodies in the little house, not enough space to make a private call. Then Gary called—on the home line, not on Stan's mother's cell—and he and Stan's mother talked and talked while Ron made up the bed in the den and settled Feldon.

One call, that's all Stan wanted. Two minutes to ask Janine a simple question. Why did you run away?

Stan was getting his room back. Ron and Feldon would sleep on the wretched pull-out that ensured guests didn't stay too long.

"If he's not gone tomorrow you're going to be reading about us in the newspapers," Stan's mother said on the phone to Gary, over and over, with slight variations, for forty-three minutes. Ron couldn't help but overhear. He kept tucking in the sheets and re-tucking and adjusting the blankets and testing the springs, like a man determined to make making the bed last as long as possible.

One simple question for Janine.

"I don't care what happens at work tomorrow! The whole office can sink into the ocean. If Ron has gone, I'll be the happiest woman on the planet!"

Ron adjusted and readjusted the window blinds, then started over again.

Finally Stan's mother got off the phone and immediately called to Stan to please help his sister with her math. Lily was still making up her own rules for addition and subtraction. An hour later she had to be stick-handled into pajamas and teethbrushing. She told him an elaborate story of the river faeries who enchanted all the fish to walk upright and wear long gowns and tuxedos.

One brief, private conversation on the phone. If

Janine liked girls the most he could accept that. He just wanted to hear it from her.

It wasn't long before Stan's mother sequestered herself in her bedroom. Ron and Feldon slept downstairs, Lily snuffled in her usual fitful state, and Stan lay in bed. Janine's damp clothes were still balled on the floor. They smelled of her. He realized he still had his father's phone. He could call her on that and yet he didn't.

It didn't feel right anymore.

He closed his eyes and in his head it was morning. Morning in a parallel universe. They were older. She was sleeping—it was the most natural thing in the world. Her black hair was a storm on the pillow. One bare breast poked above the blanket.

A line just popped into his head.

One bare breast above the blanket.

And the next line came pulling along.

One soft sigh on the shadowed wall.

It was sounding . . . like a poem. An entire poem just fell out, pre-formed.

. . . and dreamy early-morning breathing,
eyelids drawn, face so fair,
as real as real though you're not there.

Stan could see it all, this parallel morning with Janine beside him in some other version of his life.

As if it would be completely natural to wake up beside a naked, beautiful person.

An ordinary miracle, somehow.

———

STAN SAID THE POEM to himself—it was just a verse, really, it would need more—over and over while the black of night turned to shades of gray. It was in his head now. No need even to scratch it in his notebook. He really ought to undress, to slide under the covers, surrender to sleep. But he'd slept most of the day and had failed to phone Janine.

Why?

It didn't feel right. He was operating on feel.

Why did he feel now as if the exact right perfect thing to do would be to get up and step away in the night and go to her? This was the moment. What had to happen between them had to be private. He felt that knowledge in his body the way he could feel the perfect jump shot starting from the ground, the rotation of the ball as it arced toward the basket.

She was waiting for him. Until now she'd done all the chasing. Now she'd run, and it was his turn to go after her.

Stan got out of bed and dressed. It was crazy,

crazy. He gathered his runners from the front hall closet, kneeled and pulled them on, then slipped on a jacket. It was going to be cold.

And there on the front porch were Ron and Feldon.

"*What are you doing here?*" Stan and his father said at the same time.

Stan backed down first. He was still the kid. Ron probably outweighed him by fifty pounds.

"Nothing," Stan said, as if he had to explain himself to this deadbeat. Then, "I'm going out."

"To see a girl," Ron said.

Feldon was bundled on the front porch bench in his jacket, clutching Mr. Strawberry, his eyes closed, head about to droop.

No way Lily would knowingly give up Mr. Strawberry, not even to a half-brother. She was going to be furious.

"If you're going out it's to see a girl," Ron pressed.

The battered brown suitcase they'd arrived with was leaning against the front porch.

"And you're running away like you always do," Stan heard himself say. "That's all you ever know to do."

Ron looked to the darkened driveway. What was he waiting for?

"I bet you didn't call Kelly-Ann," Stan said. "I bet you lied about that."

"I told you. She's a certified lunatic," Ron said. "Like most women."

He was an old gray bearded man making pronouncements. Was this the same guy who drove Stan to the dock all those years ago?

He was waiting for a taxi.

"Look around you. What do women really want? To get their nails in you. Nails in flesh. Either you're running at midnight chasing some scent, or you're breaking their grip, trying to get your flesh free."

It was almost as if he'd been waiting on the porch hoping the taxi would be delayed so he could unload this bag of misery.

"Why did you never call me?" Stan said.

Ron bit his lower lip and shook his head almost imperceptibly.

"You got a phone to Lily somehow."

"Look. You were always on your mother's side. If I'd tried to get in touch with you, your mother would have . . ."

The thought died in the night.

"You know the thing I wanted most in life?" Ron asked. "Music. Probably I never told you. I used to play the sax. There was a group of us in high school—

the Shades. Tony Claremont, he's a recording artist now. Check the liner notes for new albums. *Tony Claremont—keyboards.* He made it, man. He didn't get bogged down with a wife and kids and mortgage and shit. He just did it. I could be there, too, if I'd stayed with it. You got something you really love?"

A gust of cold wind rattled some leaves across the porch. Winter soon enough.

"Basketball," Stan said.

"Basketball!" Dismissal dripped from the word. "You're like, a point guard or something? Can you shoot?"

His father was taking Feldon in the middle of the night to stay one step ahead of Kelly-Ann. This old gray man with the paunch who used to play the saxophone when he was in high school.

"Yeah, I can shoot," Stan said.

It was all a matter of feel.

Suddenly Stan knew what to do.

"Why don't you leave Feldon here?" he said. He crossed his arms but kept relaxed. He might need to knock his father's knee out from under him.

"Leave Feldon here?" Ron smiled madly.

"You don't want him weighing you down when you're trying to establish yourself," Stan said. "You'll be a lot quicker on your own."

It was as if pictures in the shadows were playing across the dim man's face. He even shifted his eyes toward the sleeping boy.

He looked like he'd been on the mat in defeat for a long time.

"Kelly-Ann's going to be here by morning," Ron said. "She's going to find the boy and I am never going to get to see him again."

The boy. The boy had a name!

Ron wiped a hand through his thinning hair.

"I'll hide him for you," Stan said. Now a light appeared at the end of the street. The taxi? Ron shifted his gaze, too. "I'll tell them you and Feldon took off—"

"Your mother would give him up." Ron picked up the suitcase and lifted Feldon to his shoulder in one decisive movement. What was Stan even thinking? That he could take on this guy twice his size?

The taxi crawled up the street.

"I'll take him to my girlfriend's," Stan heard himself say. "She's got a great family. He'd fit right in for a couple of days. It won't take you longer than that to get established, will it? You'll be set in three or four days?"

Give Feldon the favor you gave to me, Stan thought. Just take off.

Headlights turned into the driveway. If Stan swept across with the kick, he could maybe catch Feldon as Ron crashed down.

Stan moved to block his dad's route to the stairs. A strong driving punch to the pit of the stomach might do it.

Stan had never hit anybody in the pit of the stomach. But he felt ready now.

"I think that's our taxi," Ron said. Feldon rubbed his eyes and looked around sleepily.

"Leave him with me. I've got the phone you gave Lily. As soon as things are settled—"

"Are you blocking my way, son?"

Thunderstorms inside Stan's body now. He was standing in front of his own father. He tucked his chin in. Battle stance. But hidden, almost nonchalant.

"Leave him with me till you're settled."

Stan heard the door of the taxi open. Just on the edge of his peripheral vision he saw the cabbie get out. An old man in a turban.

"Did someone call for a taxi?"

"Leave Feldon here," Stan whispered.

Know the outcome of the battle beforehand. Know in your mind you're going to win. Then it won't matter how much of a beating you take. You'll keep going till you've achieved what has already played out in your own mind. That's how determination and bloody-minded effort overcame size and weight and years and everything else a father might have over a son.

A shitheel, cowardly father with both hands full. Both knees exposed.

"Taxi for you, sir?" the driver said. He was halfway up the walk now, but Stan could sense the man was wondering what he'd stepped into this late at night.

Stan didn't let his eyes waver. It was Ron who looked away first.

"Does your girlfriend . . . does she live around here?" Ron asked.

"A couple of blocks. They're a great family. Her father is an investor, very wealthy. Beautiful mom. They're good people. They can keep a secret. You're right, I was just going there now. I was going to see my girlfriend."

Stan reached for Feldon, who turned to him. How much did he understand?

Stan pulled the boy from his father's grasp. It's what you did with cowards. He stepped aside so the coward could have a clear path to the taxi.

"Is it morning?" Feldon asked sleepily.

Stan had him two or three paces off the front walkway now. Plenty of room for Ron to pass by.

"Just sleep," Stan whispered.

Ron, his father the coward, handed the brown suitcase to the taxi driver, shuffled his old gray self into the back of the vehicle and said something to the driver. Bus station? Train station? Somewhere on the edge of the highway?

Stan didn't want to know.

"Where's Daddy going?"

"Your mommy's coming soon to pick you up," Stan said.

Feldon buried his face in Stan's shoulder.

How much of this scene would he remember? When he got to be Stan's age, would he play it over and over again in his head?

The taxi backed out and headed away into darkness. Stan stood with the boy in his arms.

What kind of father abandons his son in the middle of the night? Just hands him over?

If he wanted out so badly, why didn't he leave Feldon with Kelly-Ann in the first place? Just out of spite?

Feldon was heavy. And he was holding onto Stan like he was never going to let go.

19

THE NEXT STEP was clear. Stan carried Feldon into the house. He would take him up the stairs straight into his mother's room and wake her up.

Wake her and tell her.

Stan's heart was drunk with it. He'd stood up to the giant! Taken Feldon from his father's arms! Without a punch, without a kick!

Just with words and with knowing what the outcome had to be.

No way Stan was going to let his dad take Feldon on the run in the middle of the night. He'd done exactly the right thing.

Now he climbed the stairs. Even with Feldon lumpy and heavy, not a sound. No creaking boards.

Sirens, practically, going off in his head. He was a man now, who used his powers for good.

His mother's door was closed. All he had to do was open it and tell her.

But his feet turned into his own room, not his mother's. His arms put Feldon in his bed again. He was going by feel.

Feldon turned over as soon as his body hit the bed. Stan pulled off Feldon's coat and shoes, covered him with a blanket. Then he walked out, stood in front of his mother's closed door.

She'd hit the roof. She'd think Ron had left another kid for her to look after. So Stan would have to tell her right away that Kelly-Ann was going to be there soon.

As soon as they could contact her.

The door was locked. If he knocked—if he whispered loud enough—then Lily would probably wake up, too.

Where was Mr. Strawberry?

Feldon hadn't been clutching him when Stan put him in bed just seconds ago. Feldon must have dropped him on the front porch. So Stan ought to go down and get Mr. Strawberry so that as soon as Lily woke up he'd have that to give her, to shut her up.

He descended the stairs again, walked out into the cold air. Mr. Strawberry was on the lawn where Stan and Feldon had been standing while the taxi drove away.

Stan picked up Mr. Strawberry, but instead of climbing the porch stairs again, he threw the doll onto the front bench.

Maybe . . . maybe he wasn't supposed to go back inside right this moment and wake up his mother and probably Lily and Feldon, too. Maybe that could wait until morning.

Maybe he had something more important to do just this instant.

———

To get to Janine Igwash—the girl whose breast peeked above a blanket in the verse now tattooed on Stan's brain—Stan headed back to the alley with the basketball hoop and the fence. Which Janine had slithered up so easily.

Stan did not slither. He was more a groaning, grasping beast pulling himself over rusted barbed wire. On the other side of the fence, in the little opening in the grubby hedge at the very back of the duplex's shared yard, Stan clumped painfully and unheroically to the ground.

There was her window. How high? Fifteen feet? Stan approached the ordinary-looking brick wall. There was no trellis to climb, no downspout that would bear his weight. A real rock climber would be able to press fingertips into the slight indentations between the bricks and become buglike in defiance of gravity.

But he wasn't a rock climber.

Stan looked around for a pebble to toss up against her window. If he moved the ladder by the carport . . .

It was quite a large one, and in his focus on looking for the stones he almost knocked it over. But he grabbed it in time and felt himself smiling, giddy. He propped it up against the wall.

Then he was just climbing up . . . a long aluminum ladder . . . in the middle of the night . . . closer to morning, maybe . . . to a point just below the window of a beautiful and fascinating girl who had kissed him.

A tilted girl. He was tilting toward her.

He was just climbing so that he would pause like this, princelike, his face about six inches from her shut and blinded window.

Was this her window?

What if Stan knocked on it now and Joe poked his big head out and punched him in the face like any father would if some guy showed up outside his daughter's bedroom window balanced on a ladder in the middle of the night?

"Janine?" Stan's voice died in the cold darkness. *Tap, tap.* "Janine, it's Stan. I'm over here, at the window!"

A breath of cold wind blew through the empty night.

"Stan?"

"Shh! I'm just outside. If you'll . . ."

She opened the window. She was in flannel pajamas.

"What are you doing here?"

The screen was still between them. Otherwise he might have just kissed her again. Probably he would have lost his footing and fallen to a spinal injury and a lifetime as an invalid.

"I'm standing on a ladder," he said.

She was trying hard not to laugh.

"I can see that."

He was freezing. The aluminum of the ladder was particularly cold. Maybe it was going to snow. The clouds had that look to them, even though it was early in the season for snow. Stan could just see some of them in the purplish night sky. Blurry cold blobs just above the lip of the roof. Dawn coming. The screen on the window, the shadows made it possible to imagine this was all a dream. In a moment Stan was going to step off the ladder and fall slowly down, only it would be like falling in water.

He'd wake up just before he hit the ground.

"I took my half-brother, Feldon, away from his

dad tonight. Our dad. I just stood in the way and took him. And now Dad's gone. I just changed Feldon's life." Stan wasn't saying it to brag. He hoped, at least, there wasn't too much bragging in his voice. He was saying it to be true.

To be true to this girl.

The screen made it seem like one of them was in prison and this was visiting hours.

"And your dad went away?"

"He's running again. That's his pattern. I can see it now. When he left us the first time, it wasn't about starting his new family. He was running away from something he'd started with us. Now he's running from Kelly-Ann. He was going to take Feldon but I wouldn't let him."

It was starting to sound like bragging now so he stopped.

If the screen weren't there he'd kiss her. Then they'd know for certain what was happening between them.

"Is your mother all right with that?" she asked. "Are you going to, like, adopt him?"

His fingers were cold anyway and he probably wouldn't be able to work the fiddly little window clasps, even if they were on the outside.

But they were on her side.

"Nobody knows yet. Feldon doesn't even know. He slept through most of it. You're the only person who knows except for me and my dad. When I was about Lily's age —" This was why he'd come, he saw it now, to tell Janine Igwash this story — "I remember sitting in the closet. The exact same closet where Lily sits sometimes now for a hiding spot."

He was doing all the talking. But he couldn't help himself.

"I was sitting in the closet when my dad flung open the door and looked in at me. He had a tennis racket in his hand and he was really mad. He said, 'Where did you put my blue striped tie?' I don't know why he had a tennis racket in his hand to ask that. Years later when he left, he took his tennis racket and a couple of bags. Mom told me. I didn't see him go, and Lily was pretty small. I remember thinking for some stupid reason, it was the tie. If only he'd found it. He couldn't have been mad for years about a tie. But I thought maybe it *was* my fault. Maybe I did use the tie for something. I used to dress up my teddy bear."

She was still at the window. Smiling now.

Maybe the dream was going to be over as soon as he stopped talking.

"But you think about stuff like that. You never

forget it. I just figured out tonight that my father is
a . . ."

The ladder shifted then, a sudden lurch to the right
as if it was going to go over. Stan grabbed the side of
the window with his right hand and his left . . .

His left went through the screen. Just pushed a
hole right through.

"Stan!" Janine grabbed his hand. The ladder
steadied.

It wasn't a dream. He was going to have to get
down soon.

"So why do you like girls?" he said.

"What's not to like about girls?"

She was holding his hand like Feldon had been
clinging to him not too long ago.

Nails in flesh, his father had said. *Either you're
running at midnight chasing some scent, or you're
breaking their grip, trying to get your flesh free.*

If the screen wasn't there he'd just kiss her and
then they'd know.

But the screen was there and he had to be careful
not to cut his wrists and bleed out in a silly death that
would maybe win some Internet award for stupidity.

Maybe he really was his father's son.

Stan eased his hand back out the jagged hole in
the screen.

"I think maybe it's time—"

"The first time I kissed a girl it was a total accident," Janine said. "It was eighth grade, right after cross-country. This girl, Idelle, she was from the Caribbean. She was really silly. We'd be running wind sprints up Criminal Hill—we had this hill behind our school and that's what we called it. We'd be running up and if you got ahead of her she'd grab your shorts. If a boy had done it I'd have hit him but none of the boys could keep up with Idelle and me. She'd reach around and pinch your nipple just when you were standing there. Then she'd laugh. Huge white teeth, and her skin was chocolate, big brown eyes. You couldn't be mad at Idelle. Anyway it was after a race, and I'd just about killed myself to get to the finish line ahead of her. I had no muscles left. And it was cold. Just before the snow. Like tonight—you must be freezing out there!"

Stan leaned toward the hole in the screen. He willed himself warmer.

"The whole team had piled all their jackets and packs and warm-ups around this big tree behind the finish line. I crawled into the pile of clothes and lay there. Idelle burrowed in right beside me. I think I came fifth. It was the best race in my whole life. And Idelle burrowed in. We were like two kids hiding in a fort. Like you in your closet. And then we were kissing. I don't know how it happened. I don't know who started it. I just remember it was like swimming naked at night. It was that perfect."

Freezing. Stan was shaking on the ladder. He wasn't sure how much longer he'd be able to stay there.

But he didn't want to go, either.

"You didn't . . . wonder what the hell was happening or—"

"We just did it. We did it and then we wondered about it later."

"And the dance . . ." he said. Was it just last night? Time was turning hallucinogenic. "When we kissed. We just did that, too. And then you ran back to Leona."

"No."

"You did! I saw you!"

"I ran but . . . not to her. I just ran."

"Why?"

Cold, cold. She didn't turn her eyes away, but she wasn't going to answer.

"You never need to run from me," he said. "I hate it."

She could unlatch the screen from her side and kiss him again. He saw now that she had to be the one to do it. It would be no good if he pushed.

"My dad's coming!" she said then harshly, and the window fell shut. Stan scrambled down three rungs so his head was well below the sill. All Joe would have to do would be to pop his head out the window, to look down a little bit . . .

Cold, cold wind. Flakes of snow bit into his cheek. He couldn't hear anything from Janine's room. Was her father there? Did she make it back to bed in time?

Should he climb up the three rungs again and see?

He didn't know.

But he did know this was no dream.

Slowly and stiffly he lowered himself down to the ground. As quietly as he could he replaced the ladder. Then he stood in the chill and watched the bruised clouds at dawn crawl across the sky.

Nothing more at her window. He could see the hole where his fist had gone through.

But then, a hand. A paper airplane glided down. A gust caught it and for a second it looked like it might end up in a tree. But it landed finally in a chilly bush. Stan reached it with just a small jump.

I like you, Stan Dart. I really do.

No signature. Just a faint image of a beautiful girl, behind a screen, watching him.

20

Six-thirty a.m. Stan ran into the gym in his street clothes and his old runners. The place was crawling with guys in shorts and jerseys, guys rubbing the sleep out of their eyes, guys who smelled already from nervous perspiration. Balls bounced everywhere, arced toward quiet hoops.

Most of the JV team from last year was there, and the ten returning seniors, and plenty of others. Just as Stan had thought, the gym was full of sweaty guys up too early, trying too hard, to fill just two spots.

Karl Brolin, Jamie Hartleman and the others had commandeered the south hoop. Like this was their private club. Brolin especially looked unconcerned, dragging his ass, slapping someone in mock defense.

Where was Coach Burgess? No time to hesitate. Stan ran straight onto the floor.

"Hey, Brolin!" The big guy didn't turn around. "One on one, right now! You and me. Game to five!"

Someone laughed. A mosquito was challenging an elephant. Brolin turned his head slightly.

"Come on! Five bucks! I get the ball first!"

Stan didn't have five bucks on him. He didn't even have his gym gear. It was all back at the house but if he'd gone home from Janine's he would have never made it to tryout. Somebody would have woken up. So he had walked and walked until the chilly dawn turned older.

"Do I know you?" Brolin asked.

"That's the fucking guy from the game," Hartleman said. "Kid can shoot."

Stan snagged a loose ball and set up just past the top of the key. "Game to five, five bucks. I don't have much time."

His mother's alarm rang at seven. If Stan wasn't on the spot to explain Feldon and the disappearance of Ron, the house might go up in a mushroom cloud.

"Where's your fucking gear?" Brolin asked. But he was smiling. He threw away the ball he was holding, took a step toward Stan. The others stood back a few steps. Stan launched a shot from where he was standing.

Swish.

"That's one!" he said.

"I didn't say we'd started yet," Brolin said. "Gotta check the ball first."

But Hartleman fired it back to Stan. "That's one, Karl! I told you the kid could shoot."

As soon as the ball touched Stan's hands he shot it again.

"Two!" he said, even before it went in.

"Kid can shoot! You got to play some D, fat ass!" Hartleman said.

Brolin walked the ball out to Stan and took a defensive stance close to him, hands ready. Angry breath. Stan motioned to shoot and Brolin rose above him like a sudden skyscraper . . . that Stan zipped around. A nervous layup. The ball circled the rim, circled . . .

"Please go in," Stan muttered.

"Three! Kid's got three!"

Everyone was crowded round now. All the other balls stopped bouncing. It was like a playground fight. Brolin shoved the ball at Stan, then slapped it away, elbowed his way to the basket. Slam dunk.

"One," he grunted.

At the top of the key again Brolin took his own long shot. What was he thinking? No spin, flat arc, clang off the rim. Stan grabbed the rebound, scooted to the corner past the three-point line, then launched another shot before Brolin got on him.

"Four! Kid's got fucking four!"

"What's going on here?" Coach Burgess said. He just materialized somehow. He wasn't a yelling kind of coach. He was worse, as far as Stan had heard—a man who never raised his voice. Never repeated himself.

"Who opened the equipment room?" he asked quietly.

Karl Brolin hung his head.

"You want to play for me, you work first. Understood?"

Someone dropped a basketball that bounced twice, like embarrassed thunder, before he could corral it again in clumsy hands. Marty Wilkens. What was he even doing here?

Burgess stared him into cold stone. Then slowly his eyes fixed on Stan.

"Where's your gear?"

Stan couldn't think of what to say.

"Anyone who wants to play for me respects this gym, respects the game."

"Yes, sir," Stan said. Then, "I have to leave anyway."

"*What?*"

"My mom gets up at seven o'clock," Stan said. As if that could explain anything.

"Kid can shoot, Coach," Jamie Hartleman said, but in a pleading tone.

"Take your disrespect and get the hell out of here," Burgess said to Stan. He turned his head slightly. "Brolin—a hundred pushups. Right now. I don't care if you die doing them. Everybody else—fifty sprints. Length of the gym. Call out your numbers."

Nobody moved.

"*Go!*"

21

"MOM?" JUST BEFORE seven Stan stood quiet as a burglar outside her door, his chest heaving. He'd run all the way home, his fifty sprints and more, fast as spit, with no one watching.

He'd just ensured that never in his lifetime would he make the senior varsity team.

"Mom. I'd like to come in."

He'd picked up Mr. Strawberry on the front porch to give to Lily as soon as she woke up.

"Stan?"

Flushing from the ensuite bathroom. Then he heard the closet opening and closing. She was looking for her robe.

When she opened the bedroom door she stood, so tired she was practically vibrating in her red satin robe. Her hair looked like she'd been clutching it and letting go all night long.

"Dad took off. I convinced him to leave Feldon with us. Kelly-Ann is coming to get him . . . I'm . . . sure."

His mother looked like she was in a dream.

"Have you been out running or something? Why do you have Mr. Strawberry?" she asked.

He told her about the taxi, about saving Feldon.

"Feldon is here?" she said.

"He's in my room. Dad was leaving in the middle of the night. He wanted to take Feldon but I convinced him . . ." It was like the remote. No matter how patiently he went over it, she still couldn't seem to get it.

"When is Kelly-Ann coming?" she asked finally.

"When we call her, I guess."

"You *guess?*" His mother looked around, lost. "And Feldon is sleeping in your bed?"

Stan took her into his bedroom to show her . . . the unmade empty bed, Feldonless.

"He *was* here." Stan knew he sounded ridiculous.

"You lost him?" Now his mother was waking up. Stan pulled back the rumpled covers as if the kid might have made himself so small he could be hiding there. Then Stan kneeled down and looked under the bed, remembering how Feldon had hidden in the kitchen cupboard just the day before.

No one. Feldon was not there.

"Your father left him in your care and you've lost him?"

"I gave him my bed and . . ." Stan didn't want to go into any further details. It was his business what he did after saving his half-brother from a wasted life with a cowardly dimwit of a father.

And what? What did you do?

He could say that he had slept on the pull-out. It was still rumpled—probably. Probably it would sound true and all he'd be then was a liar.

"Mr. Strawberry!" Lily blurted and launched herself at Stan. "You found him!"

Her pajamas were soaking. Stan could smell it almost before—

"Lily! Oh, God, Lily!"

Lily started to just scream in the middle of Stan's room with Mr. Strawberry wrapped around her neck.

"Stop screaming!"

Stan moved quickly to carry off the kicking girl. She screamed and screamed directly in his ear, and pounded her fists against his back, but he held on until she was simply sobbing against him.

"It's all right. It's all right, sweet knees," he whispered to her.

He carried her downstairs. A sign on the toilet, in his mother's hand, read FLUSH AND I WILL KILL YOU. Stan filled the tub for Lily, who started shrieking again until she couldn't catch her breath anymore. Then Stan handed her a warm washcloth so that it became more or less all right.

Stan's mother burst into the bathroom holding a reeking wad of Lily's sheets. "Lily, where did Feldon go?"

"Feldon is gone?"

"It's all right!" Stan said quickly. "Dad's gone again. But I made sure he left Feldon. But we don't know if Dad came back in the night to get him?"

Why hadn't Stan paid more attention? It would be just like Ron to change his mind in the taxi and come back and steal Feldon away.

"*Lily!*" Stan's mother said.

"Feldon would have told me if he was going anywhere." Lily splashed quietly now, not looking at either of them.

"What I'm saying is that last night Dad was going to take Feldon away. They were both going to leave in a taxi . . ."

"But where?"

Someone knocked on the bathroom door. "I need to go pee-pee!" said a little voice.

Stan's mother ripped open the door. Feldon was standing in his clothes—the ones from last night—holding himself and doing a little dance.

"*Oh, for God's sake!*" Stan's mother said.

"Feldon slept with *me* last night!" Lily said.

"*I have to go!*" Feldon danced and held himself.

"Well, I don't want to see your nib thing!" Lily yelled back.

Stan took him to the upstairs bathroom.

"It stinks in here," Feldon said, but Stan got him to plug his nose.

"I thought you were gone!" he said.

"Lily came and got me," Feldon said, his pants around his ankles.

"Lily did?"

"She saved me from the taxi man." When Feldon turned around to explain he almost sprayed Stan, who stepped deftly.

"Keep your eye on the bowl there, big shooter!" Stan felt like laughing. "It wasn't Lily, it was me, Feldon! I was the one who saved you last night."

———

THERE WAS NOT MUCH time now to explain it all again to Stan's mother, to get her to understand. Some things she grasped much better than Stan, but they tended to be old things. Mortgages. Finances in general. Love, probably—although Stan was beginning to see that even now she hardly understood anything about it, and that was a sobering thought. The woman who had married Ron did not have a firm grasp on the most important human endeavor.

Love.

Love was the most important human endeavor. Stan could see that now, too, even as he was explaining Feldon's presence and Ron's absence yet again to his mother, who was running around in her bedroom looking for a clean outfit to wear to what might be her last day of work.

It was Monday, the day of the all-staff meeting when something extraordinary was about to be announced—extraordinary but probably not good. Good would have been announced on Friday, so they would all have had the weekend to celebrate. So probably bankruptcy, funding pulled, or some other collapse.

"I have to go! I have to go!" she said, fiddling with her earrings. She was constitutionally incapable of stepping foot outside the house before she'd re-applied her lipstick. If it was going to be the end she'd look well put together at least.

Stan felt like he could look at women differently now. Not long ago he had stood on a ladder clutching the wall of a woman at a very odd hour before sunrise.

"Today of all days I have to go and simply can't look after Feldon!" she said.

"I'll stay with him," Stan said.

"You have school!" She was changing her earrings now. She had a very female way of cocking her head while putting on earrings.

She was exchanging black for white—beads for pearls. She was a good mother. He felt calmer just watching her.

"You can't just skip class to babysit," she said. "I'll call Kelly-Ann from work. She must be out of her mind with worry."

"I don't have anything big today," Stan said. "I've got all my textbooks at home anyway. I'll just work from here." He felt calm. A windless lake at dawn. The man who was up 4-1 on Karl Brolin before Coach Burgess walked in.

"You had something on today," she said. Shoes now—the black or the beige? Height or comfort?

"Nothing. It's all review."

A narrow escape, now that he thought of it. Who would ever want to play for Coach Burgess?

She went for height. Black went with pearls. Then she changed her belt—a smaller silver buckle for her skirt. She hadn't had breakfast yet. How often did she leave home just like this, in a panic, without breakfast?

"You had something special today," she pressed. "What are you forgetting? I know you told me!"

She stopped to look at him. Gary was stuck on her. That's why Gary was hanging around. He wasn't much to look at but he could spin a ball into a hoop backwards with people watching.

"It's a nothing day," Stan said. "You call Kelly-Ann. I'll look after Feldon. So go. Go!"

"But . . ."

"I'll get some breakfast into the kids and Feldon and I will see Lily to the bus."

22

"ONE WOBBLE OVER this line," Lily said, "and the goblins start to burn. Just like flies when you put them under a magnifying glass."

They were at the bus stop. Lily was pointing with her toe at a squiggle in the dirt by the curb. "But all they want to do is get over that line!"

"Why?" Feldon asked.

It had turned into a brilliant, bright morning, the air cool, the world unusually fresh. None of the snowflakes from last night had lasted.

"Because that's what you do when you're a goblin. You try to get over the line!"

The bus pulled up and she climbed on board. She did not look back at Stan or Feldon.

"She wiggles in bed," Feldon said on the walk home.

Stan picked up his ball at home and took Feldon to the back lot, where he showed his half-brother the basics of the set shot. The ball was too big for Feldon's hands but he could still bend his elbows and knees properly and line up his shoulders and use the whip-wave of his body to propel the ball high enough — and cock his wrists to spin it after follow-through. The spin was so important.

Stan chased down rebounds and demonstrated different shots. Feldon stayed with it for a while. Then he got distracted by some ants that were staging a battle on a perfect square of ancient patio stone that someone had abandoned near the fence. Red vs. black, millions of them having it out. Feldon squatted to be closer to the action. The battlefield remained precisely within the boundaries of the patio stone. No ants stepped beyond, although they could have — of course they could have.

It looked like the black ants were slightly bigger than the red and were carrying off their opponents' bodies in surging columns. Eggs were being carried off, too. There beyond the patio stone, in a long line that Feldon followed. Stan sat on his basketball and listened to his explanation.

"Goblins are waiting for them in the cracks. That's why they stay on the square. Except the egg line. Goblins hate eggs." He said it like a future neurosurgeon.

People were going to listen to Feldon, Stan thought. People might never believe Lily, but Feldon they would listen to.

And Kelly-Ann was coming any moment now to take Feldon away. The thought came to Stan suddenly, like sitting on a bruise he'd forgotten.

"Your mother is coming to get you," Stan said on the walk home.

"When?" Feldon asked.

"Soon, I think." The basketball fit like the whole world under Feldon's arm. "But we're going to stay in touch."

"Will you come visit?"

"Yup. We'll just figure out when."

"And we could go fishing?"

Had Feldon really enjoyed fishing?

"Anything you want. We're half-brothers. We can do it."

Stan was going to get his driver's license soon. He could go visit whoever he wanted.

He wasn't a kid anymore.

———

AT LUNCH THEY WERE dipping soldier fingers of toast into soft-boiled eggs when the phone rang. Feldon had yellow egg yolk dripping from the corner of his mouth, which Stan was about to wipe. Instead he walked to the phone. Probably it was Kelly-Ann, insane with worry about her son.

"Hello," he said calmly, and tossed Feldon the kitchen rag.

"What are you doing home?" Kelly-Ann said in a very familiar way, as if . . . as if she was actually Janine, not Kelly-Ann.

Stan's heart bounced like a basketball.

"I'm looking after Feldon."

"Jason Biggs said you ran out of tryout," she said. "And you missed biology. Stillwater said anyone absent was going to get zero."

The test! Stan had completely forgotten.

"Did Biggs say I didn't miss a shot?"

Feldon munched, munched his toast soldiers. The sun was slanting and even through dirty windows half of Feldon's face was in shadows, half in bright light.

"What happened?"

So Stan told her all about it, and the rest as well—his mother, the dramatic day at work. It was like he was back on the ladder again. The world didn't matter. It was just . . . great to have her to talk to.

"Are you worried about your mom?" Janine asked. "What if she loses her job?"

Stan wasn't worried . . . because of the way the sun hit the egg yolk that was still on Feldon's face. It was hard to explain beyond that.

"Whatever happens is just going to happen," he said. "It's just a problem."

"Of course it's a problem! If your mother loses her income, and your father won't help any . . ."

"No, I mean, it's *just* a problem," he said. What did he mean by that? The words slipped out. He would have to think it through later.

He had the sense that a lot of what had happened recently he'd have to think about at another time.

Feldon was nearly finished his soldiers. Stan checked the milk in the fridge. It smelled all right. His mother needed to do a proper shop for the whole week, not just grabbing stuff as she did from time to time on her way home. How much was in her bank account? He had no idea. But they were still going to eat. Weren't they?

"Some things there's no solution for," Janine said.

He pictured her standing outside the school doors, the phone pressed against her left ear. He thought about leaning in and kissing the base of her neck. Just where the lizard sat.

How warm it would be.

"If you're home alone looking after Feldon then maybe I should come over." She said it just like that. *Maybe I should come over.*

Maybe this was where she was supposed to be.

Stan felt calm and yet his pulse steamed, as if he was driving for the hoop just a half step ahead of Karl Brolin.

"Come on over," he said to Janine.

———

COME ON OVER.

"A friend of mine is coming over," he said nonchalantly to Feldon as he stood over the sink and scraped at the egg on the plate and the cutlery.

Maybe she could come over and Feldon might fall asleep and one thing might lead to another. Maybe he'd have a chance to lean toward the heat of her body—he could feel the heat of her, just thinking about it—and maybe he could . . .

Feldon was folding a business reply card from a magazine that had been on the counter. Tiny, precise movements.

Future neurosurgeon.

Confident fingers. The card was turning into something intricate.

"Where'd you learn to do that?" Stan asked.

"My mom showed me."

"Really? She's pretty smart, I bet."

Tiny, tiny folds. Feldon kept his eyes just inches away. Like a scientist looking through a microscope.

A bunny, maybe, with pointy ears? Feldon compressed it with his finger and it hopped.

"Amazing!"

Feldon set the paper bunny on the counter angled toward the door, as if it might scamper off any moment. He found a coupon in a pile of papers and began to fold that.

"You must miss her?" Stan said to Feldon.

"Who?" the boy asked.

"Your mother!"

Fold after fold.

"She can do butterflies," Feldon said solemnly. "And Uncle Liam can do dragons!"

"Who's Uncle Liam?"

"He comes to help Mommy sleep. But he has to leave really early. Sometimes he makes bacon."

"He helps her sleep?" Stan said.

"When Daddy isn't home."

The doorbell then. Stan felt a surge—Janine!— but summoned all his powers to ignore it.

"What do you mean? How often does your dad go away?" *Your dad.*

"Only sometimes," Feldon said. "This time he brought me, too. Maybe Mommy won't be home."

The bell again. Stan saw Janine through the blurry front door window.

Janine Igwash in his house.

"Why won't your mom be home?"

Feldon started folding something else from the pile of papers. "Because she went to Me-too Bay."

"Where?"

Stan got up to let Janine in. There was an awkward moment at the door when really all he wanted to do was kiss her deeper and deeper for about half an hour until they both melted from the heat of it. Instead he stood too far back with his hands in his pockets, shuffling his feet.

"Hey," she said.

She was crackingly beautiful.

Somehow Stan remembered himself.

"Me-too Bay?" he said to Feldon. "What?"

"That's where she went," Feldon said.

———

MONTEGO BAY. That's what Feldon was trying to say. It took a while for Stan and Janine to get the information out of him. First he had to tell them all about the new bathing suits that kept arriving in the mail and how his mother would stand in front of the mirror and turn this way and that but she couldn't decide on pink or black. And every suit made her look fat, she said. And Uncle Liam would tell her she wasn't fat and she would say she was and he would bring home pie for everyone.

Janine helped Feldon arrange the folded creations, some of which looked like animals and some were just shapes. Janine sat with her legs crossed and her body inches away from Stan.

"Is Uncle Liam her brother or—?" Stan pressed.

"He's her sleeping friend," Feldon said.

All the folded creations were facing in the same direction, like cows in a field.

"He snorts pretty loud," Feldon said.

Janine's collar cut across the little lizard. It was an effort to keep himself from reaching out to touch it.

"And he makes funny noises in the bathroom."

Stan laughed too loud. The air in the room was nearly boiling just because Janine was sitting there.

"And now your mother and Uncle Liam have gone to Montego Bay?" Stan pressed.

"Sometimes we went to the go-carts," Feldon said.

"He let you drive a go-cart?"

"*Brmmm! Brmmm!*" Feldon said. He turned his hands as if he was steering.

"But what was your dad doing while all this happened?"

"*Brmmm! Brmmm!*"

Feldon was as bad as Lily. Stan put his hand on Janine's shoulder, and she melted into the movement.

"Where's your dad's bedroom?" Stan said finally to Feldon, who squinted as if this was the most ridiculous question. "I mean, do your mom and dad . . . Do they sleep together, or does he have his own place?"

Feldon squealed, it was so funny. "Daddy doesn't sleep! He works!"

———

HOW SOME PEOPLE arranged their lives—good luck trying to figure it all out, Stan thought.

But maybe . . . maybe his father had good reasons to leave after all. It was hard to grasp what the situation might be. Stan wasn't in his father's shoes.

But he wouldn't have abandoned his son, that was for sure.

Stan and Janine took Feldon to the park and

played on the swings with other preschoolers. Janine asked Feldon if he went to kindergarten and he acted as if he'd never heard of it. He dug in the sand with his fingers and moved twigs and rocks into position so that the hole was surrounded by a barricade. So the ants wouldn't get in.

Two or three mothers eyeballed Stan and Janine for looking too young to have a kid themselves, Stan guessed. But it was no one's business. Janine lifted Feldon and hugged him for a moment before putting him on the high swing. She would make a terrific mother, Stan thought.

Feldon ran up and down the tall slide and Stan wondered what they were going to do with him if Kelly-Ann didn't show up. What if she stayed in Montego Bay—in Jamaica!—with Uncle Liam, drinking fancy drinks and lying on the beach? What if Stan's mother really did lose her job? What if something burst inside her from the pressure and she had to go to the hospital to die, leaving Stan in charge?

What would he do?

Stan watched Feldon run down the slippery steel. What kind of kid refused to slide? Janine was beside him, letting him do it. He was going to fall and break his front teeth and the other mothers would just cross their arms and say, "What are you doing having a kid at your age anyway?"

"Hey, Feldon, let's go home, buddy!" Stan said suddenly. He clapped his hands like he was somebody's coach. "Hey, Feldon. Stop running!"

"It's okay," Janine said.

Feldon was going to break his head on the steel post.

"Stop it!" Stan yelled.

The boy twisted, lost his balance. Stan lunged, caught Feldon by the arm, braced him with his body . . . and barked his own shin on the edge of the slide.

Stan said nothing, just held his half-brother and carried him down to the ground.

"Are you all right, buddy?"

Feldon squirmed, trying to get back on the slide.

"Let's head home, okay?"

"He was all right till you tried to grab him!" Janine said.

A whole crowd of mothers was looking at them now — teenagers with a child.

Stan didn't trust himself to speak till the wave of anger had passed.

Janine was looking so beautiful, it hurt not to touch her.

It was just a wave.

But he could see how a man could lose control and screw it up because of a wave.

Everything was tilted. The whole way home he felt like he had no idea what the next step might bring.

23

FELDON NEEDED HOT chocolate and a marshmallow. It was a minor miracle that both were in the cupboard. The marshmallows were particularly rocklike, but they melted in the hot drink.

There wasn't enough mix for Stan and Janine to have hot chocolate, too.

No messages on the answering machine.

Stan's mother had not come home yet, so maybe the office was not shutting down after all. Stan imagined if the place was going bankrupt or otherwise falling apart then everyone would be sent home early, like with a snow day at school.

He was going to have to get a note to explain his absence from school. Beg for a chance to write Stillwater's test.

Feldon showed no signs of running out of energy.

He wanted them all to play hide-and-go-seek, which meant he would hide and Stan and Janine would count and then stumble around the house calling his name. Janine kept bumping into Stan—in the hallway, in the den, on the stairs. Her thigh would angle against his, or she would touch his arm for a moment or put her hand on his hip, not quite on his rear but not far from it, either.

Feldon hid in the linen closet, under the master bed upstairs and under a blanket beside the sofa. Each time they let him go for longer and longer while they sat in the living room on the loveseat, quite close but not touching, not really. Stan counted out loud and Janine looked at him, and Stan looked at her.

He didn't really believe she was there. It seemed like another trick of the mind. He wanted her so badly and here she was.

Dark eyes.

Heating the whole world.

Finally they found Feldon semi-snoring in the same cupboard in the kitchen where he'd hidden the other day. His chin leaned against the edge of a pot and Stan tried to extricate him gently, but he was not moving.

"Do you think he can just stay in there?" Janine asked.

They were both on their knees looking in the cup-board. Her mouth was so close to his that he had to pull back to miss it.

Her hand was on his thigh. For balance.

"Can't be very comfortable," he said.

If she pushed slightly she could knock him flat on his back.

"I'd love to see your room," she whispered.

If he tried to get up too quickly the blood would evacuate his head and he might keel over into the sink.

No dream.

He closed the cupboard door gently and pressed forward on his knees so that she had to kiss him. Which she did, kneeling on the floor, until the universe dried up and both of them nearly spilled into the legs of the kitchen stools.

"It's up the stairs," Stan said finally.

His room, he meant.

She reached between his legs, which was not far at all.

"Feels pretty tight," she said. She had a gentle way of squeezing. So Stan reached between her legs but she intercepted his hand.

"Upstairs," she whispered.

The blood left his brain long before he stood.

They walked together up the loudest set of cracking stairs ever built. Where was Stan's weight? He had no idea. His feet were somewhere miles down below the rest of him.

Feldon did not wake up.

This was all part of the dream. She knew exactly where his bedroom was. She'd seen it during hide-and-go-seek. He followed her like a balloon on a string.

She pulled him through the door.

And closed it behind.

She looked at him and didn't do anything, really. But somehow buttons began to undo themselves and Stan's shirt fell from him like old skin. She had old skin, too, to lose but first he needed to escape from all of his.

She pulled it from him.

He probably should pull hers.

But he was on the bed, being propelled backwards. She was pushing him backwards.

She wants this, he thought, a slow-motion realization. She wants this as much as I do.

Maybe more.

"It's beautiful," she said. "You're beautiful."

Meaning all of him, not just the throbbing egomaniac in the center.

He wasn't particularly calm. Somehow her shirt came off and in bending forward for something — just to kiss his belly, actually — the pink lace fullness of her bra brushed against . . . things and he spurted like a fountain. Like some Yosemite geyser on a nature show.

All over her beautiful chest.

"I'm sorry! I'm so sorry!" he said, and when he got up he was still gushing — on the bedspread, on her arm, the carpet, the floor.

"Is that . . . ?"

She didn't complete her question. It was all new. New in fact but he could tell she knew the facts.

The facts of life.

Sixteen-year-old boys were lousy lovers.

Stan pulled a reasonably clean gym sock from his drawer and wiped the milky glue from himself.

Then he pulled out a T-shirt — exactly the same T-shirt he would have worn to the basketball try-out that morning if he had remembered to pack gym gear — and wiped what he could of the rest, from Janine and every other object he'd sprayed.

"I had no idea," Janine said. She kept sneaking peeks at him. He was still naked and . . . and rigid as ever, practically. Grinning, one-eyed fool. "I had no idea it shot out so easily."

She was in her bra and her skinny black pants and there was the lizard tattoo waiting for him to kiss it.

"It has a mind of its own," Stan said.

He wrapped the gym sock in the T-shirt and placed the whole disgusting wad carefully, dry-side down, on the carpet by the bed.

He started to pull his underwear back on.

"Are you finished already?" Janine didn't sound disappointed. All right, she sounded a bit disappointed. But mostly she just seemed to be asking.

"I'm going to be oozing for a while," he said.

He pulled on the plain old, baggy, ripped white cotton underwear he'd owned since he was eleven.

"Those are cute." It was a cool thing to say, but Janine's face was baking red. She wasn't looking away. She didn't seem to be going anywhere.

———

IT WAS LIKE SWIMMING. In the warmest, most delicious water. Underwater sometimes, but with clear vision. And breathing. And being able to fly and being underwater all at the same time.

He wasn't sure always when he was inside her. *Inside her!* It was clutch and accelerator. It was taking a shot to win the game from too far away but it didn't matter.

It was some of those things.

It was completely different.

Sometimes he was inside her and he didn't even know it. Or he felt like maybe he was inside her but he wasn't sure. When he was on top he was more certain—if she put him there.

Sometimes she put him there.

Sometimes . . . sometimes he wasn't sure where his skin ended and hers began, because it was terrifically hot, and he was sweating like the hottest day in the hottest gym, but it wasn't that. It was sweat so hot they steamed together with the touch of her belly . . . of her belly sliding against his . . .

They slid.

There was no talking.

Sometimes she whispered something, but it wasn't . . . words so much as . . . little exclamations and low noises.

And her hair kept brushing against his skin . . .

The lizard tasted salty.

They kissed and kissed just like in the kitchen but even more so.

It was all for real.

He had a vague sense that she might get pregnant.

But probably she wouldn't. He'd already fired across her bow. It was a funny saying. He started to laugh for a moment until she asked him what was so funny, and then he couldn't say, and she started doing something . . .

There was a lot they did together.

Everything.

Everything changed on the little rectangle of his bed on a slow afternoon with Feldon sleeping downstairs in the kitchen cupboard and Janine Igwash swimming in his arms, and he in hers, until her hair was stringy wet and his skin was completely . . . completely new and even then they kept kissing to make the planet stop.

The whole planet stopped.

That's how deep, how impossibly, they kissed.

24

STAN WAS LOOKING AT POSTS — slow, self-painting posts — but Janine was on the dock. Lying in the sun.

She was so much in the sun that he could hardly see her. But it looked like . . . she was in a bikini, maybe, and her eyes were closed so he could watch all he wanted.

If only he could see her better.

"Stanley!"

It was fascinating to watch the thick white, glossy paint creep up inch by inch, post by post all by itself.

"Stanley!"

His mother's voice.

"There you are!" She was barging through the door, eyes first . . .

"What are you—! For God's sake, Stanley!"

At least Janine wasn't there, he thought. It was all just his usual dream.

"Who the hell is that?"

Janine turned, sleepily.

Oh, shit.

"Mom—"

"Stanley! Stanley!"

The furious recitation of his name.

"I left you in charge—!"

She didn't know where to put her eyes. Stan had the pillow now in front of himself . . .

"Oh," Janine said.

"Where the fuck is Feldon?" his mother said.

"Mom, it's all right." His heart was pounding in his brain but he felt calm.

"Where did you put him!"

Stan put his hand on Janine's shoulder. She was trembling in the sheets.

"Give us a minute," he said, dead calm, a whole expanse of desert in his voice. "Mom, this is Janine. We'll be out in a—"

Another voice said, "Who's that? *Oh, my God!*" A woman was peeking around the door—big glasses, mousy hair. *"Oh, my God!"* she said again and disappeared, but her voice rattled in the stairway. *"Feldon! Oh, honey—Feldon!"*

"Is that Kelly-Ann?" Stan said, stupefied.

"Get yourself together!" Stan's mother hissed and ran out of the room, clacking in her heels, slamming the door.

"*Uhnn,*" Janine said under her breath, like she'd been punched in the stomach.

Stan knelt beside her and gathered her in his arms.

"Listen." His hands were shaking, too, but he didn't feel that way inside. He felt like he was on the bridge of a battleship somewhere. That he had huge forces at his command.

"Listen. We're going to get dressed and go downstairs. You're my girlfriend. I love you. And my mom is—"

"*Feldon! Where are you!*" Kelly-Ann screamed downstairs.

"Is she—?"

"Feldon's mom, I guess," Stan said.

He tried to kiss her but she pushed him away.

"Now your mom is going to hate me." She whipped her bra on like she'd been practicing for years. Stan rooted amongst the tangle on the bed, on the floor. His sorry underwear again. He found a new shirt and his old jeans. The battleship feeling receded and his head felt light.

"Stanley! Stanley!" his mother screamed, probably from the kitchen. *"Get down here now!"*

Janine raced into the rest of her clothes.

"I'm going to go," she said, scared. Stan took her shoulders again. He was only half dressed, but they'd shared everything.

Everything.

"Stanley!" his mother screamed.

"I love you," he said.

———

DOWN THE STAIRS. Stan held her hand.

His girlfriend's hand.

"Mom," he said in the kitchen. "This is Janine Igwash." He meant to give some kind of apology — an apology that actually was no real apology, more like an admission of the excruciating embarrassment of this particular moment caused by . . .

He waited for the words to assemble themselves. He thought of his mother racing off as a young woman to her military lover's apartment in the fifty-five minutes after sociology, at the same time that she was supposedly going out with the man she would stupidly marry.

How to put everything in a few sentences, and

not only in front of his mother and Janine but Kelly-Ann, too, this mousy woman whose face was shock pale—hardly the look of someone who had just been on the beach in Montego Bay with her own lover?

All these thoughts, and what came out was, "He's in the cupboard."

Right beside where his mother was standing.

"He fell asleep in the cupboard!" Stan said. It was impossible to keep the anger from his voice. Because of the way they were looking at him—at him and Janine, as if they'd been off screwing around or something while Feldon wandered away.

No one moved so Stan reached past his mother and opened the cupboard door.

"He's right . . ."

But Feldon wasn't there.

"I'm going home now," Janine said. "Nice to meet you, Mrs. Dart." She even extended her hand, which Stan's mother looked at like it was diseased.

Janine bolted down the hall.

Stan stood dumbstruck, still looking in the Feldonless cupboard.

"I'm calling the police," Kelly-Ann said.

She seemed older than Stan had expected. Not as old as his mom, who dyed her hair . . .

"I'm sure he's around . . ." Stan said. Kelly-Ann

had her cellphone out. Then he said, "I'm sorry. I'm so sorry. He really was dead asleep . . ."

Why did he use the word *dead*?

"You left him asleep in the cupboard?"

Kelly-Ann was on the verge of shredding him.

Stan's mother gripped his shoulders now. "What time did you leave him? Stanley! *What time!*"

He didn't know. Time seemed irrelevant, at the time. He remembered the kiss, which was endless, on their knees in front of the cupboard door.

"We were playing hide-and-go-seek," he said.

"Bullshit you were!" his mother said. "I know exactly what you were playing!"

Kelly-Ann got through to the police.

"My little boy has disappeared," she said, real fear in her voice.

Stan heard himself sound exactly like Ron. "I'm so sorry. I didn't mean . . ."

Any of it.

"I was visiting my sick uncle at Mitou Bay," Kelly-Ann said on the phone. *Mitou Bay!*

Where the hell was that?

Not Jamaica.

The cops were never going to understand even the simplest aspect of all this. Stan hardly understood it and he'd been there for a large part.

"No. No. I don't believe my husband took Feldon . . ."

Kelly-Ann was shrinking in the kitchen, trying to summon help.

"We are estranged. Yes. He's a pathological liar. He took the boy to his ex-wife's home . . ."

Stan's feet started moving. Out the kitchen. Out the front door. Down the steps . . .

"Stanley!" his mother called. "You come back here! The police are going to want to—"

He had to make things right.

———

HE RAN AND HE RAN IN the heart of the afternoon with the already low slanting light of fall easing into winter. He ran as if Coach Burgess were watching, clipboard in hand, estimating his character. As if Janine were with him, the wild girl with the strong stride. As if he had to keep up with her, impress her somehow, be worthy. He ran as if he wanted to stay by her a long, long time.

He ran to the only place Feldon could be—where Stan's feet knew to take him.

Down by the river. That's where he would go if he were Feldon.

And that's where Feldon was. Squatting by the edge of the greenish brown water, his hands on his kneecaps, eyes so serious. Neurosurgeon.

The big fishing rod was lying on the bank behind him, unused.

"Hey!" Stan said, breathless but still strong.

Feldon didn't get up, but his face lit and Stan felt suddenly that they really were brothers.

"The fish in here swim backwards!"

Stan kneeled beside him. "Backwards?"

Feldon pointed. The fish was hardly a minnow, almost invisible in the murk, especially in the low slant of the sun. It was sliding backwards.

Slowly, slowly.

"Your mom's here," Stan said.

Feldon was mesmerized by the water.

"She's pretty worried about you. I think we should go back to the house."

Not a movement. Feldon's eyes were fixed, his body quiet and still.

"I'm going to come visit you," Stan said. "No matter where you end up living. They can't keep brothers apart."

Feldon nodded. He took a bit of grassy fluff and dropped it in the slowly moving water.

"Here, fishy. Have some lunch."

The fluff floated off, swirled around a rock, got pulled into the main channel.

Feldon stood up finally. "I have to get off my feet," he said with great seriousness.

"Do you?"

"To make a jump shot," he said.

———

ON THE WAY BACK Feldon talked a lot about the fish.

"He wanted to have lunch but he couldn't get to the top. Maybe he can't swim very well. He's just learning."

"Maybe the current was pulling him backwards," Stan said.

A police car raced past them with siren screaming. Feldon looked up, unconcerned. It seemed to be heading in the direction of their house.

"Where's the girl?" he asked.

"What girl?"

"The big girl."

"Janine's at her house now," Stan said. "I'm going to call her later. A whole lot of dust needs to settle first. But I'm going to call her right after."

Another police car whipped around the corner and sped past them, lights flashing, siren on full wail. Every car all the way up the hill homeward moved over to make room.

"You should bring her some flowers," Feldon said.

"Flowers? Really?"

"Girls like flowers." Feldon scrambled up a low wall off the sidewalk toward some patch of garden Stan had never noticed before. It was the front lawn of the seniors' residence across the street from Long-worth Mall.

"I don't think you should be picking those." But Feldon went ahead as if he'd heard nothing. Yellow ones, some purple, others that were not quite red. What was the color? Russet.

In very short order Feldon had put together a decent bouquet.

"Girls really like flowers," he said again.

The Tilt-the-World groaned in the parking lot across the street. Hardly anyone was on it, and yet it just kept going.

A third police car screeched past, bound for hell up the hill.

"Maybe we should go see Janine first," Stan said. "I could phone home from there." He wanted to see her again right away. Let her know it was all right.

"Maybe she could give me some more hot chocolate," Feldon said.

They were walking again. Heading home.

"Her mother's got cancer," Stan said. "She's dying."

"Where will she go then?" Feldon asked.

"I have no idea," Stan said.

"Maybe when you die, that's when you learn how to use your tail and your fins," Feldon said. "You can go up to the top and have lunch."

"You've really been thinking about this," Stan said. The sun was so low the sky looked metallic, like a photograph in a glossy book. The silver beast tilted but just for a second the world stayed steady.

"Not really," Feldon said. "I just now thought of it."

Slowly, slowly they walked up the hill. Stan was mesmerized by all of it—from the slant of the light to the beauty of the traffic to the bittersweet feel of every step.

I'm going to remember this day for the rest of my life, he thought.

Then, only a few steps later, his stomach clenched around one particular thought.

Where did it come from? Why this instant?

Why did he suddenly know that today was the day he'd got Janine Igwash pregnant?

25

PREGNANT. Why hadn't he realized it before? Because he'd been in a dream, a stupid, thoughtless state of addlement. But now he was waking up.

Janine Igwash was pregnant. By him.

Why?

He'd sworn he would never be here. He was not going to become . . .

His fucking father.

"You're hurting my hand!" Feldon said.

He was holding Feldon's hand. Feldon had the flowers. Stan had the fishing rod.

"Sorry," he said.

It didn't even sound like his voice.

In Family and Sexuality class, Mrs. Hardon had said sperm needed only the slightest invitation to cause irreparable parenthood. Even if you'd already . . . shot across the bow. There was still sperm in the nozzle.

Lurking.

He was nothing but the agent of his own nozzle.

"We're not going to see Janine right now," Stan said.

Instead, the flowers were for Kelly-Ann.

It was a touching scene. The house surrounded by cop cars, lights blazing, Kelly-Ann scrambling off the front porch—Stan thought she was going to trip and break her neck—then hugging Feldon so hard he yelled in alarm.

Stan's eyes welled up. He didn't know what was happening. He didn't get weepy about anything, usually. But the sight of the little boy squirming, of Kelly-Ann nearly killing him with her own relief . . .

Stan, too, was going to be a parent. It just kept hitting him, one load of bricks after another. He'd have to leave school. He'd have to get a job, in a brick factory, probably. He'd be moving bricks from one place to another. Probably by hand. He didn't know anything else.

He'd have to learn that, even.

He'd have to support Janine and the little baby. And his mother would be alone with Lily. His mother and Lily would unravel each other. And Stan would come home to Janine—to some filthy little apartment they couldn't afford—after a long day of moving bricks, his arms stretched from the weight of it all.

Janine would look at him with that face mothers get, that end-of-the-world face.

He'd come back to his crying kid and his unraveling wife—her parents would probably make him marry her—and they'd be together in a squishy, filthy, stinking, dark peeling-paint apartment . . .

Desolate in the driveway, Stan gazed at Kelly-Ann Wilmer clutching Feldon and weeping. Everyone was weeping.

Stan wept for himself. His blood was turning to chalk.

He might as well call himself Ron.

They were all a huge public spectacle—cops, neighbors, Lily home from school, his mother. Lily was wandering around in circles talking to invisible people at her toes.

"He was just down at the river," Stan said to nobody at all. No one was listening to him anyway.

———

DINNER WAS SOMETHING from a box that went in the microwave and then came out hot and mushy. The colored parts were vegetables, Stan guessed. The whitish-yellowish parts were pasta. Gary poured wine for everyone—even Stan—except the children, who got berry juice.

The wine sat murkily on Stan's tongue, like some token of the adult world that was hard to appreciate. Gary went on about—vintage, mustiness?—while Stan considered brick dust filling his lungs.

"To life!" Gary said, and everyone clinked. Stan's mother was looking at Gary like . . .

"I have a word to say about life," Gary said.

. . . like he was a Greek god or something.

"Some days," Gary said, "you lose your job." He looked over at Stan's mother. So that was it. How were they supposed to live? But Gary was looking at her like she was the greatest thing since . . . "Some days you get accepted into a special school—" Gary glanced now at Lily chopping her mushy noodles into smaller and smaller bits—"or you lose your kid, then you find your kid."

Kelly-Ann had Feldon on her lap, clutched like he was a parachute she hadn't strapped on.

"It all could happen on the same day. What's important, what really stays with you . . ."

Is what your nozzle caused you to do, Stan thought.

" . . . is all of us together. I don't care what any-one says, we are . . ."

Just agents of our nozzles, Stan thought. Our nozzles and our appetites.

" . . . a family," Gary said. Some kind of eye-based tractor beam vibrated between him and Stan's mother.

"I know this has been a tumultuous day . . ."

They were getting married, Stan thought.

" . . . but I would like to make an announcement. Isabelle and I have decided—"

"I got my girlfriend pregnant!" Stan blurted. That stopped the words in Gary's throat.

"*What?*"

"Janine is pregnant," Stan said. "She's my girl-friend. It's my fault."

Stan's mother crashed her cutlery on her plate. Everyone else was silent. Even Lily looked up.

"Oh, Stan," his mother said in a little voice.

Freight trains collided in his ears.

Why had he said it? Why had he said it out loud?

Gary still had his mouth open, but nothing was coming out now.

Welcome to the family, big fella, Stan thought. Welcome to the nut house.

"When . . . when is she due?" Stan's mother said.

"Have you talked to her parents? Has she considered . . .?"

"It's all really new!" Stan sprang to his feet because he had to, his whole body uncoiled. "I don't want to talk about it."

Up the stairs. To hell with the squeaks. A huge storm seemed to be blowing all around him. He launched into his room where it had all happened, where his life had come peeling apart in a matter of minutes.

Why?

Because he was Ron's fuck-up son.

There was the bed, sheets and blankets still wrapped in knots. That's where the disaster had unfolded. It was like he'd been on drugs or something. He'd gone completely out of his mind.

There was the balled-up T-shirt-and-gym-sock combination on the floor. Why hadn't he just stopped there? Obviously he was unfit for . . .

But Janine had wanted to go on. She'd never tried boys. She didn't know what she was doing.

But it was his fault. He knew himself.

He thought he knew.

He buried his face into the wreck of his bed. Everything was cold now. Cold and dark. It was difficult even to remember the steam heat of it.

"Stanley." His mother's voice.

"I closed the door for a reason!" Stan barked.

Everyone else in the family was allowed to come apart. Everyone else could slam the door and be left alone. But not him.

Why didn't he have a lock on his door?

"Don't come in!"

But she came in anyway, bearing food. Cold microwave mush. She sat on the edge of his bed—the very scene of the disaster—and put the ridiculous plate on the floor right beside his smelly wad of disgrace.

He could hear her sniffing distastefully.

"You really need to do your sheets," she said.

He didn't have to talk.

"I'm sorry for this afternoon," Stan's mother said. What was the phrase? Eggshells. Eggshells in her voice. "You know, as a parent, sometimes you get completely blindsided by something. You just . . . barge in with the current crisis in your head, and you have no idea. I'm sorry."

If he kept his head in his pillow she would go away eventually.

"Janine seems like a nice girl."

If he stayed still as a corpse . . . if he *became* a corpse. If he willed all the life to drain from his . . .

"I mean, it was a horrible way to meet someone. I wish you had brought her to dinner first or something. I have asked you many times if you're seeing someone. I know we're a bit chaotic as a family, but—"

"I wasn't seeing her!" Stan said. "We just got together. It's all really new!"

That shut her up. Stan waited, but he couldn't continue to be a corpse. He shifted to look at her. Shades of gray in the darkness.

Something in the bed was still slimy from . . .

"How new is it?" she asked finally and pressed a little closer. Her hand was going to touch the slimy part . . .

Stan sat up completely in a protective posture.

"Just today. We just started everything today. When you walked in . . ."

"Oh," she said. "Just today?" It was as if she was sitting in the den with the three remotes, indiscriminately pushing buttons.

"*You walked in on us!*" Probably everyone was lined up on the stairs listening.

"How do you know that she's pregnant?" his mother asked.

"I just know! I'm Ron's son, all right? I've got this—"

"Did she tell you that she's pregnant?"

"She didn't have to! I didn't use any protection, I didn't think . . ."

Slime, slime still on the bed. It was disgusting. Stan couldn't ignore it anymore. He wiped his hand against something unusual . . .

"What's that?" his mother asked.

It *was* slimy. But it was also slippery and sort of like a—

"It's a condom," she said. "It's . . . it's . . ."

Slippery in his fingers.

"*Huge!*" she said.

Stan dropped the thing. It looked big enough to . . .

"I thought you said you didn't use protection?" His mother didn't seem to know where to put her eyes.

"It's a girl's . . ."

"A what?"

"A girl's condom," he said. He'd seen pictures of them. In health.

"Janine wore this?"

God. How could he not . . .

The thing lay there like a squishy plastic bag.

"Anyway, if you just made love this afternoon, there's no way she could know that she's pregnant. No way. And if she wore this . . ."

She was brilliant, Stan thought, and it all slid

from him—the brick factory, the lung dust, the shitty apartment, the hard weld of his jaw—

Everything flooded.

"Oh, Stanley."

Flooded into his mother's arms. He felt himself shaking against her chest, weeping like a baby. She held him and stroked his hair.

"Oh, my baby," she said in a whisper. "You're only sixteen. It's all right. You don't have to know everything."

How could he miss-see so many things? How could he go through the whole sweaty passion of it and not even know?

"I think you should bring her to dinner. When everything has settled."

"Are you and Gary going to . . ." He could barely talk. He was just weeping and breathing.

"We'll talk about it. I have to find work now."

Weeping and breathing. She smelled good, his mother. In the face of his unbearable stupidity . . . he didn't want to let go.

"It's all right. I think it's good," he whispered. Footsteps on the creaking stairs melting away. All of them. The drama was over for now.

Stan held her and held her until the world calmed down.

26

A JUMP SHOT STARTS IN the soles of the feet and travels, like a wave, up through the ankles, shins, knees, thighs . . . through the hips and up the spine and out the arm and fingertips. It happens before thought travels through the brain. The ball spins nightward . . .

. . . toward the hoop in the back alley, where the beautiful girl slithers up and over the fence and emerges from the darkness before the ball clangs against the rim.

"I got your package," Janine said.

She was wearing the plaid shirt and jeans he'd returned. He could see the shirt under the opening of her leather jacket. She had the coolest clothes. She filled them out a lot better than he had.

Stan grabbed the rebound and dribbled twice,

spun the ball in off the backboard, dribbled to the foul-line crack, sank a jumper, sped in before the ball could even touch the ground . . .

"You wanted to see me," she said.

She had her hands on her hips. Even in the dull light she shone like the most brilliant beauty ever to set foot on an improvised back-alley basketball and martial arts court.

It wasn't quite raining and it wasn't quite snowing. The air seemed full of the turning of the season.

"One bare breast above the blanket," he said. "One soft sigh on the shadowed wall. And dreamy early-morning breathing, eyelids drawn, face so fair, real as real though you're not there."

She didn't move.

"I am real, and I am here," she said finally.

"It's not finished yet," he said.

"Is it a poem? Is it for me?"

"I need to kiss you again."

"What for? Research?"

She would not smile at her own joke. He got the flowers then from the shadows. That seniors' residence garden had a good selection. It was almost winter anyway. He brought them to her.

"I don't really like flowers," she said.

"I thought all girls liked flowers."

He could see her breath. That's how cold it was getting. Not that he felt any of it. She sniffed the flowers even though she didn't like them.

"My mom does, though. She'll carry them with her all over the house."

Their noses were almost touching. He had to crane his neck upwards.

"I'm a troublemaker," she said.

They stood in the cold, dull light for the longest time, just heating up the whole world.

"You *are* a troublemaker," he said finally. He wasn't going to make the first move. They stood nose to nose attracting one another. Her lips parted a little bit. He could smell her . . . was that lipstick?

Something fell in the tiny space between their nose tips. A snowflake?

Hours could go by like this. Eternities. Just breathing the same air.

"Your mother must hate me," she said.

"My mother has asked you to dinner," he replied. "I have to warn you, the family is infested with liars and fools. But you have to come."

She could . . . she could just stand there breathing and keeping her lips half a thought away. He leaned in slightly but got no closer.

"I'm not my father," he said then.

She didn't ask what he meant. They didn't need to talk really. Slowly Stan began to get the sense that two people standing like this, so close together, with so much between them . . .

Maybe better not to say it. To just let the world fall to bits around them in the most delicious ways.

Acknowledgments

THE AUTHOR GRATEFULLY acknowledges the financial assistance of the Canada Council for the Arts, the Ontario Arts Council and the City of Ottawa in the preparation of this manuscript. Thanks, too, to Shelley Tanaka for fitting both her considerable heart and head under her editorial hat in steering me through various drafts, and to my friends and colleagues at the Vermont College of Fine Arts, especially Louise Hawes, whose brilliant lecture on desire set this story in motion. Many thanks as well to publisher Patsy Aldana, my agent Ellen Levine and to other friends and family, whose comments and suggestions were so helpful.

About the Author

ALAN CUMYN IS THE AUTHOR of many acclaimed novels for both children and adults. *The Secret Life of Owen Skye* won the Mr. Christie's Award and was nominated for the Governor General's Award, the Ruth Schwartz Award and the Pacific Northwest Libraries Association Young Reader's Choice Award. *After Sylvia* was nominated for the prestigious TD Canadian Children's Literature Award, and *Dear Sylvia* was shortlisted for the Canadian Library Association Book of the Year for Children Award. Alan is also a two-time winner of the Ottawa Book Award, and his novel *The Famished Lover* was longlisted for the Giller Prize and the International IMPAC Dublin Literary Award.

Alan teaches in the MFA program at Vermont College of Fine Arts and is a past chair of the Writers' Union of Canada. He lives in Ottawa.